BOOKS BY MARY ELSIE ROBERTSON

Speak, Angel   1983
The Clearing   1982
After Freud   1980
Jordan's Stormy Banks and Other Stories   1961

Speak, Angel

Mary Elsie Robertson

SPEAK, ANGEL

ATHENEUM NEW YORK *1983*

With gratitude to Yaddo and to the MacDowell Colony
for time and space in which to work.

LIBRARY OF CONGRESS CATALOGING IN PUBLICATION DATA

Robertson, Mary Elsie, ———
  Speak, angel.

  I. Title.
PS3568.O2497S6 1983   813'.54   82–73015
ISBN 0–689–11362–5

Copyright © 1983 by Mary Elsie Robertson
All rights reserved
Published simultaneously in Canada by McClelland and
Stewart Ltd.
Composed by Maryland Linotype Composition Company,
Baltimore, Maryland
Manufactured by Fairfield Graphics, Fairfield, Pennsylvania
Designed by Mary Cregan
First Edition

For Joe Chris.
And for Donna.

NOVEMBER

Burl

ALL he had to do was say he had to see the dentist. Toothache. He went up to Jim at twelve, when the whistle blew, catching him half in and half out of his office. "Looks like I got to take off awhile this afternoon," Burl told him. "I got this tooth's giving me fits."

Jim didn't even look at Burl, his mind clearly elsewhere.

"When you reckon on getting back?" That was all Jim said, and Burl marveled at how easy it all was.

"Two-thirty, maybe. You ever go to the dentist and know how long it was going to take? Once you're in there they got you by the balls, don't they?"

Jim laughed in that dried-up way he had. Not laughter with any pleasure behind it. He waved Burl on with his hand.

Burl congratulated himself as he ran through the parking lot, dodging the handles of cars. It was a cold, fall day, good hog-killing time if he was down home. He saw it clearly—the sharp bristles sticking up out of the rolls of white fat, and the tiny purple hole at the side of the hog's head with black powder marks around it. His daddy throwing the curled-up tail into his lap once—that was when Burl was just a kid—and laughing when he jumped up, yelling with fright to have that thing touch him.

"Know what that is, Sonny? That little ole curl?"

"It's his tail!"

"Naw. That idn't no tail. That's his squealer."

"Not no squealer!"

"Why, if it idn't his squealer, what'd you do just now? Didn't I hear you squeal to beat the band? That's his squealer like I told you."

Burl laughed now, at the joke, cutting between a Cutlass on one side and a Camaro on the other. He hadn't appreciated his daddy as much as he should have when he was a kid, but kids were like that. There were a lot of things they didn't have the sense to see until later.

He swung up into the cab of the pickup and slammed the door. He enjoyed it up there, sitting high above the cars, like he could drive right over their tops which would cave in like tin cans. The first thing he did when he settled behind the wheel was to reach over to the glove compartment and run his fingers over the gun, the metal cold as a frog's nuts.

It wasn't until then, while he was gunning the motor, that he knew he'd been a dumb fool letting Jim know the hour and the minute, giving him all the necessary information so it wouldn't take the sheriff more than about ten minutes to find out he hadn't gone to a dentist at all that afternoon. He might as well stick a little sign up by that haircutter's body saying "I was the one that done it. Burl A. Trotter."

But how long would it have taken anybody to figure it out, anyway, with the motive clear as glass? He hadn't ever been one to hide, and he wasn't concerned about getting caught. That part hadn't ever concerned him. It was the way he'd always been, going after what he wanted without a look to either side, like he was wearing blinkers. Same as when he'd started busting broncos and riding bulls when he was a kid. Everybody told him he'd get himself killed. Even his daddy hadn't been too enthusiastic, though he had ridden in rodeos himself when he was a young man. Of course he'd gotten himself busted up. He carried one leg now that was an inch shorter than the other, and would go on carrying it until the day he died. "You seen me limping around here ever' day of your life. Looks like you'd pay a little heed," his daddy had told him, but he hadn't done it. Nobody could talk him out of a thing he had his head set on. His momma had worn out a maple tree in switches on his legs when he was little enough to switch to good account. But he always did what he was determined to do. He went on riding in rodeos until he got stomped on by a Brahmin bull in Fort Smith that time and decided on his own accord he'd probably had enough. But he had to make up his own mind about it. If you started listening to what other people said, pretty soon they would be running your life instead of you running it yourself. And he'd a lot rather make mistakes along the way than let that happen. He wasn't ashamed of a thing he'd done and not sorry about a one, either.

Only there was something about the way he'd moved out on Lenora that didn't sit too well with him. Somehow he hadn't handled that right, but go over it as he would he couldn't figure out what it was he was supposed to have done.

He pondered this over again as he eased the pickup out of the parking lot and headed for the thruway. By rights she should have been the one made to leave the house since she was the one in the wrong. But then, he couldn't have kicked the girls out, never mind the boys. Scott and Jeff felt like strangers to him, now they'd moved out of the house. But then, he'd been the same. At sixteen he was already riding the circuit—Texas, Arkansas, Oklahoma—one fairground like another, and when he was at home in Pea Ridge, he was working at the cannery in the summers. So he knew how it was with Scott and Jeff and didn't hold it too much against them. But the girls were different. They were just eight and eleven and needed somebody to look after them. Most people would say that person ought to be their momma. But Burl thought sometimes that maybe he ought to have taken the girls too when he left. He shouldn't have left them there to see what their momma was up to with that haircutter. Charles Van Hopper. That Dutchman or whatever fool kind of a name that was. A man with a face like a piebald horse.

When he got along about here in his deliberations, he came to the question of whether or not he ought to shoot Lenora at the same time he got that haircutter. For a while he thought he would. She deserved it as much as the man did. Maybe more. But the quarrel, it felt like to him, was between men. It was like Lenora was outside the whole thing. But of course that didn't make any sense. Lenora was right in the middle, that was where Lenora was. So he couldn't decide about it. Sometimes he pictured the haircutter lying with a purple hole in his head, looking up at the ceiling, and Lenora cowering against the headboard, her pointed face turned to him, her mouth open a little, the way she'd stood at the edge of the ring watching him ride bulls back in Pea Ridge.

But as soon as he pictured her face the way it had been then, pointed like a flower, her hair catching the sun just like gold, his heart drew tight and he could feel the pain of it drawing up like a fist. She could still do that to him, after all those years they'd been married.

The part he liked to think about best was coming in on Lenora and the haircutter. Stealing up the stairs, careful to skip the ones that creaked. Not making a sound as he sneaked up to the door of the bedroom, the gun a good, satisfying weight in his pocket. His fingers circling the door handle, holding it tight the way his fingers would fit around a person's Adam's apple if he wanted to crush it in his hand. He'd turn the handle slow so they wouldn't suspect a thing. And then he'd push open the door and stand in the opening. They'd see what they were in for, all right, and no mistake.

That was the moment he looked forward to—the one when they saw him, and realization came over their faces. Their mouths would drop open, their eyes shut tight in fear. He'd stand there a long time, letting it sink in, before he would slowly draw the gun out of his pocket and raise his arm.

It was what followed he wasn't so sure about.

Sometimes he thought maybe that was all he wanted. To catch them in the act and hold the gun to their heads, showing them what he could do if he wanted to.

But other times he was pretty sure he wouldn't stop there, just holding the gun on them. Once he had them like that he wouldn't be able to stop himself. He'd even enjoy it—shooting that hair-cutter and watching him keel over there in the bed.

As he came off the thruway and entered the country, passing the long flat fields bordered by huge trees made vigorous by the winter snow they had to endure, he rolled down the window and let the air blow in. Heavy, damp air full of the smell of rot from cabbage stalks not yet turned under in the late-fall plowing. In all the time they'd lived up there in New York, he hadn't gotten used to this countryside. It could still take him by surprise and make him wonder how come he lived in it, though he'd left Pea Ridge, Arkansas, of his own sweet will. But the older he got, the more often certain things about the country around Pea Ridge came to his mind. That thin soil down there that kept the trees to a reasonable height but gave enough scope for the honeysuckle and blackberry and sassafras. He could picture in his mind the dogwood in the spring, picking out the woods in white. And there was his momma standing on the porch in the twilight, looking down over the spring woods. "If I could write a poem I'd tell the world what that looks like, now," he could remember her saying.

"You could if you wanted to, Momma," he'd told her, scuffing his toes along the porch. But he knew she couldn't write a poem any more than he could. Something caught at you sometimes, making your heart hurt with the need to tell, but there weren't any words that would come to you.

That was the way this thing with Lenora and the haircutter made him feel, now he came to think about it. What they'd done drove him nearly crazy. It drove him so crazy there wasn't any way he could tell someone else just how he felt about it. All he knew for sure was he wanted to kill them.

It came over him strong—some song going through his head—and when he put his head back and let it out, pounding on the steering wheel for the rhythm, it was "Will You Be Loving Another Man" that filled his throat and mouth. "Will yew be lov-in' another maaan . . ." Well, she would of course, did of course, love another man. And he would take his revenge the same way all those other husbands did in song and story. He knew what to do.

It had been two weeks since Burl had been down the road to the farmhouse he and Lenora had rented together, and now he slouched in the seat, hoping not to be seen. Still, he knew people didn't pay as much attention to their neighbors here as they did in Pea Ridge. His momma saw nearly every car or truck that passed by the road in front of the house, but then, it was the same people living in the same houses for years. Up here people moved around more. He and Lenora had only been in the farmhouse since summer, and he knew nobody took serious note of them.

Before he got to the house he turned off on one of the roads that cut along the edge of the fields— onto one of the roads used for tractors. There were so many trees and bushes bordering it that he didn't think even now, with most of the leaves gone from the trees, the truck could be spotted from the house. He could see it, though, through the bare limbs. No way to tell from this distance whether or not Lenora and the haircutter were in the house together, but he wasn't about to tip his hand by driving past to see if Lenora's car and the Lincoln were in the driveway side by side.

Burl parked the truck, took the pistol from the glove compartment, and slid from the seat onto the road.

His lunch was still sitting on the seat in a paper sack. Since he hadn't bothered to take it with him into the plant that morning, he must have known all along that this was going to be the day he'd go to the farmhouse. Leaning over the seat, he reached into the bag and retrieved the apple from the bottom. He wasn't sure if he was hungry or not, but he thought he ought to eat something. It's not a good idea to kill somebody on an empty stomach. It seemed to Burl that his daddy had once said something like that to him, though it would be a strange thing if he had, because Burl was sure his daddy had never shot anybody in his life. As a young man, riding in rodeos and working on the railroads, he'd been a brawler known for his hot temper, but Burl didn't think he had ever killed a man. By the time Burl had come to know him, his daddy had calmed down a lot and taken to going to church—to the Freewill Baptist up on the highway. At night before he went to bed now, his daddy read a little bit of the Bible to himself, holding the book tight in both hands and moving his lips over the words.

The best thing, Burl figured, would be to come up on the house from behind. The barn would block him from sight most of the way, and after leaving the shelter of the barn he could circle around the garage and come up on the house from its blind side. The boys would be at work during the day, over at Tony's Highway 36 Car Repair. They wouldn't be in the room they'd fixed up to live in above the garage.

He walked fast down the road, biting into the apple as he went, liking the sharp clean sound of the cracking flesh. It satisfied him—the way the juice spurted between his teeth.

Crossing the field, walking down the row between the stalks where the cabbages had been cut— some whole heads left to turn a mushy brown—he took big strides, measuring his legs against the roughness of the ground. It had been a long time since he'd walked across a plowed field, and he enjoyed the way his heels sank at every step, breaking through the crust the fall sun had made.

It was a funny thing to him that he'd been the one wanting to live in the country, and yet he was the one who'd moved into that dump of an apartment on Howard Street back in the city. He was the one always talking about going back to Arkansas or Texas. Someplace where they could buy some land and raise Black Angus cattle. Someplace where they could have horses. The boys had been all for it when they were growing up, but he didn't know about the boys any longer. The girls, though, kept asking when it was all going to happen. They had names for their horses already picked out. When the girls were little enough to sit on his lap, he used to tell them about riding in the rodeos and

showed them his thumb that got bent the time he
fell off his horse and landed on his hand wrong.
They were always after him to tell them stories like
that.

But Lenora turned up her nose at the mention
of going back South to live. "What's there to do
out there in the country?" she was always asking
him. "Sit on the front porch and watch the traffic
go by, like our folks do? That what you've got in
mind? I thought you wanted to get away from all
that."

"Listen," he told her, "if we had horses we
wouldn't have time to sit on the porch. We'd have
horse shows to go to." He could see it, each mem-
ber of the family sitting astride a palomino with
saddle shining. The girls in cute little cowboy
boots and hats, their ponytails rippling down their
backs.

At the corner of the barn Burl stood with his
shoulders back against the wall, easing his head
around it the way people do in movies. What he
saw was the sweep of the driveway, which was
empty. So Lenora and her boyfriend weren't there
yet. Or maybe they'd left their cars in front of the
house. Although he didn't think this was likely, he
didn't want to take any chances, so he skirted between trees and came up behind the garage. From
there he could see the whole of the front yard, and
it was plain there were no cars parked there either.
It made him feel low, that emptiness. It wasn't
until then, as he stood at the corner of the garage
and looked toward the house, that he knew how
much he'd counted on Lenora and the haircutter
being inside the farmhouse.

He came from behind the garage and stood in

the driveway wondering what to do next. But there seemed nothing to do except stare at an old Thunderbird sitting up on blocks in front of him. Rust had gotten to it bad, and more was wrong with it too. A valve and ring job, he remembered Scott saying. Transmission. Brakes relining. The boys had picked the car up for two hundred dollars, towing it home behind the pickup. He understood what they had in mind, how they saw themselves driving that car down the road with all the rust sanded away and a new, shiny paint job. But Burl knew this wouldn't come about. All around the car the ground was littered with tools the boys had dropped when they got bored.

The boys had always left their bicycles out for the rain to fall on, and the garage right now was full of skis with broken bindings, ice skates without their mates, mangled minibikes. The boys insisted that they were going to fix all this stuff that was broken and then they'd sell it and make some money. But with every move more of the junk got left. Behind them, every yard was littered with broken things.

Burl had to admit that some of this waste was his own fault. Lenora had always told him he spoiled the boys, and he admitted it. Growing up without two dimes to rub together, he hadn't been able to say no to his boys, not if he had money in his pocket. When they were little, the things they wanted hadn't cost so much—$7.98 for some game they'd seen on television, or $11.95 for a cowboy with movable arms and legs. Later on, though, he'd gotten into the expensive stuff—skis, minibikes, equipment for every sport known to man. But none of it had held the boys long.

Crossing the driveway, Burl kicked some kind of wrench far under the car. It made him sick to see all that stuff getting ruined. He came from a household where even string was saved. His mother worked the knots out of it and rolled it into a ball which she kept at the back of the knife drawer. Not a thing went to waste in that house, but not one bit of that carefulness had come down to Scott or Jeff.

He'd been lax too long. He saw that now, when it was just about too late. It was the same thing over Lenora and the haircutter. If he'd let Lenora know right away he wasn't having any, then it could all have been stopped, early, before anything much got under way. The very first time he happened to drive past the Grand Union and caught a glimpse of Lenora leaning into the window of some strange car—a fancy one, a Lincoln—with her skirt hiked up in back and her elbows on the rolled-down window, her face not five inches from this man who was smirking out of the corner of his mouth, he should have told her right then that he wasn't having any.

But he hadn't said a word to her at the time. And all he said later when she got home was "Saw you with your skirt all hiked up, laughing your fool head off with some fruitcake in a Lincoln. Nobody *I* ever saw before."

Lenora got all haughty, the way she did sometimes when she thought he was acting like a hick. "That, for your information, was Charles Van Hopper. Charles of the Mr. Charles Salon in the mall. Eighteen fifty for a haircut. Fanciest place in town. If I could get taken on there I'd probably make twice as much as I do with Betty."

"And that's what you were talking about? A job?"

She cut her eyes away from his so all he could see was the line of her eyelids, flattened out. "Sort of. Sort of talking about that."

"I bet you were. In a pig's ass."

"What do you think, Burl? I can just go up to Charles Van Hopper and say 'I'm Lenora Trotter, you know? And I was just wondering if maybe, if you had any openings right now, I could get a job with you'? Is that the way I ought to do it, according to you?"

Right there was where he ought to have pushed it. He could see it now. But he hadn't done it. He'd backed down. He could just see himself, looking down at the linoleum and saying, "Well, I don't know anything about that haircutter and I don't want to know anything about that haircutter. But what he looks like to me is something you'd use to mop up the floor with."

"I guess it's my business where I work. Don't you think I've got sense enough to get myself the best job I can?"

So of course he'd just let the thing drop. He'd given her a free rein, you might say. Even though he knew now—nobody had to tell him—it had been a mistake. If he'd told her right then and there that money didn't count and if he saw her once more with that Mr. Charles or whatever he called himself she'd have the print of her teeth set in her lip for good, then that would have been the end of it. But he hadn't done it, and now it was too late.

When he came to think of it, he saw there were just two places he'd been weak—two places where he hadn't been the kind of man he ought to be, the kind of man he was most of the time. One of the weak places was Lenora, and the other was the boys. Maybe he'd been weak with the girls too, but he wasn't so sure about that. It was all right for a daddy to indulge his girls. But he'd acted like a fool with Lenora and hadn't done what he ought to with the boys. They were spoiled and Lenora was spoiled, and if something was spoiled you had to get rid of it. He could remember very well helping his momma carry off the spoiled cans of corn from the pantry. The tops and bottoms of the cans got so rounded they wobbled on the shelves. You had to be careful taking them to the garbage heap or they'd explode like bombs.

Burl had the key to the house in his pocket. He'd carried it around with him ever since he'd moved out, because he'd known all along he was going to use it one day to get back in that front door.

The house was a mess. That was the first thing he saw. Nobody had touched the place for a week, looked like. Beer cans lined the windowsills. Somebody had spilled coffee on the living-room rug, and the stain had spread, dark as blood, to the leg of the sofa. Dirty dishes rounded the sink. Half a stick of margarine lay mashed on the kitchen table.

Burl went carefully up the stairs, stepping around one of the girls' Barbie dolls where it sat, its legs sticking out in front. Although it was wearing a skirt, its top was bare. Burl looked at it for some time, disturbed. It seemed to him it might be a message of some kind, his girls trying to tell him something, but if they were he couldn't figure it out.

The door of the bedroom he had shared with Lenora was closed, but he pushed it open and went inside. This room, he saw with bitterness, was orderly. The bed was made, the floor vacuumed. In the middle of the headboard, sprouting from a brass stem, was a lamp he'd never seen before, one with a frilly shade and a little red glass ball like a cherry screwing it into place. When he clicked the switch the light shone pink and the red ball glowed.

He could imagine the way that light would fall on their bodies—Lenora's and the haircutter's—making them look smooth and young. He clicked the lamp on and off several times, getting the effect. It was a strange thing, but the picture of Charles and Lenora naked together in bed had not come clear in his mind until that moment. He had not imagined the haircutter's red lips, as full as a woman's, cruising over Lenora's breasts, had not seen his dark head between her thighs. And now those pictures assailed him as though their bodies lay before him on the bed.

His knees felt suddenly weak and he sat on the edge of the bed with drops of sweat rolling down his ribs. He hadn't seen it before. All he'd had was the thought that Lenora was two-timing him. But now he felt his stomach turn to water. Not until that minute had he known how deeply he'd been injured, how he'd been gut struck and hadn't even felt it. That heat gathering behind his eyelids, that rising of bile in his throat, was murderous rage. He'd seen it before in the eyes of bulls battled to a corner of a pen before the holding strap could be gotten on them. That pinpoint deep in the eyes that meant they didn't give shit about death; killing was all they cared about.

He had to lean for support all the way down the stairs and out the same door he'd come in. But he'd get himself through the yard, across the fields, and into his truck if it took him two days. He was going to sit out there until Lenora and that haircutter came to the house, and then he was going to get them.

Adele

Adele's math paper fell out of her English book as she slid into the aisle of the bus and she saw it being slipped backwards along the floor, from shoe to eager shoe, while she stood there with rage boiling in her chest. She knew it would be Donny Schultz who would grab it off the floor to wave above his head, and of course it was. Donny with teeth pointed like a weasel's.

The bus was stopping, and if she didn't get off fast Mrs. Strasser would get mad again. "You better give it back to me," she yelled at Donny. "I have to get off here. You know good and well."

Donny waved her paper in the air, whistling through his teeth as she struggled toward him with arms all along the aisle of the bus reaching out to grab her. It was because they hated her, for some reason. And up in front Mrs. Strasser honked the horn, *hoot, hoooot,* mad the way she always got when there was trouble on the bus and she didn't know what to do.

"Come and get it!" Donny called, waving her paper like a flag, and all the others took it up too. "Come and get it, get it," so the bus seemed to rock with the noise. Mrs. Strasser was honking and Martha was pulling on her skirt to come on, come on. She ran pushing against all the arms—nothing would stop her getting back what was hers if she had to break every arm like a stick—and snatched the paper from Donny's fingers. But he wouldn't let go and she heard the paper tear. It wasn't fair at all. It was mean. Tears came to her eyes, but she wouldn't show it. She'd never give them the satisfaction. She hoped Donny would die. She hoped something terrible would happen to him and the school bus would roll right over his head and smash it the way some boy smashed the jack-o-lantern she and Martha made at Halloween. The pieces lay all over the steps, yellow mush.

But the paper was in her hand as she and Martha ran down the narrow metal steps, the door of the bus closing behind them nearly on their skirts, making a hissing noise. She heard the final click as the door shut and the bus pulled away, carrying with it the smell of gasoline fumes. And then she and Martha were in the driveway under the bare trees where the light was so deadened under the thick clouds it was like being under a hand.

Adele shivered, tipping her head back to look at the sky. Her throat hurt as though she had just been screaming for a long time, but it wasn't the swelling in her throat that made the stillness come over her as she stood in the driveway. It was something else. It was the heavy way the clouds pressed down. It was the empty house that seemed to watch.

The house had seemed friendly in the beginning

when they first came, all of them crammed into the car. They had driven up the driveway under the trees thick with leaves, and through the open windows came the smell of grass.

"I told you, didn't I?" Daddy said. "Didn't I always tell you we'd live in the country?"

"But the ponies," she wanted to know. "Where're the ponies?"

"Not yet," her father said. "Later, maybe."

That first afternoon when they came to the house they trailed through the rooms together, full of excitement. Her father and mother talked about how they'd paint and paper the rooms. They were planning to stay in the house for a long time and it would be like their own, even though they were only renting again. But they were together, just the family, with all that space around.

The boys went off by themselves to hang out the upstairs windows and smoke, and Adele and Martha climbed over the broken wall behind some trees and slid to the bottom of the hill where an animal had made a wallow. The grass was mashed down where some heavy body had rolled from side to side, and the crushed grass spread from that one place the way hair grows on a person's head. She and Martha sat on their heels, side by side, with their arms around each other's shoulders. Through Martha's shirt she could feel the bones poking, arching like the wings of a bird. She liked it there in the hollow because it was a secret place. Blue flowers grew in the grass, and white butterflies with small black dots on their wings fluttered uncertainly from flower to flower as though they were absentminded and forgot, in midflight, where it was they were going next. She and Martha giggled because nobody in the house knew where they were hiding.

In the beginning the farmhouse was the best place they'd ever lived. For one entire day they'd worked together, even Scott and Jeff, cutting the grass, hammering down loose boards on the porch. And they were going to do lots of other things too. Plant flowers. Fix up the barn so somebody might want to board horses there. That would be a cheap way of having the pleasure of horses without the expense, their father said.

That summer the whole family ate supper together outside, under one of the big maple trees, late in the afternoon when the boys came home from work. They ate tomatoes and corn on the cob and hamburgers cooked on a grill, the meat laid carefully on the rack when the charcoal glowed red-hot. Adele thought they looked like families she had seen in magazines, all smiling as if something wonderful was about to happen.

She looked at her mother and father and Scott and Jeff and Martha, all sitting under the tree in the sunlight, as though she were taking a picture with a camera. In a frame made by her hands she saw the bright light and laughing faces and shut out the shadows from the trees. It wasn't at all like one of those pictures that Jeff had taken a while back with the camera he got at Christmas. Somehow too much light got in his camera, so the people in the pictures seemed to be ghosts with soft, blurred features. It was hard, in those photographs, to tell her from Martha, or Jeff from Scott.

But the picture she saw of them sitting under the maple tree was bright and clear to start with, and the faces were laughing. Later, when she thought of the picture again, she saw that changes had been made. Then she could see that there were shadows at the edges of the picture after all. First they were hardly noticeable. But they reminded her of the blotches that marred the mirror Grandma Trotter had on the dresser in the back bedroom of her house in Arkansas. When you looked at yourself in that mirror, part of your face appeared to be blotted out. The black part was eating right across the mirror, through all the silver. Pretty soon, when you looked, there would be nothing of you left. The blackness would have taken you away.

"Come on, Adele. You aren't going to stand in the driveway all afternoon, are you?" Martha said, yanking her toward the house. So of course she couldn't. It was too cold to stand outside anyway.

She knew it was only something she was making up—that the windows of the house were eyes watching them. The house was only a house. Yet she always hated that first minute when they pushed open the door and went inside.

She was the responsible one, the one with the key. So she reached to the bottom of her jacket pocket while Martha hopped from foot to foot in the cold, ready to push into the house the moment Adele turned the key in the lock.

At first, when she shut the door on the cold, she was relieved. But as she eased her books onto the bench by the door, even before she took off her jacket, she felt her heart start to gather speed under her ribs. She felt it powerfully—that they were not alone. Someone had passed through the room. She was nearly certain the chair that usually sat by the couch had been moved aside. The rug

had not been bunched at the edge when they left
for school that morning.

She grabbed Martha's hand to hold her where
she was. A murderer could be hiding in the kitchen
or on the stairway landing.

The house was very still. She could hear no
sound except a dog barking a long way off. The
light was dim because of the heavy clouds.

"What is it?" Martha said.

But she shook her head, saying "Shhhh," very
softly.

"Somebody's in here," she whispered, forming
the words slowly with her lips so that Martha could
read them.

When the fear leaped into Martha's eyes, as
Adele knew it would, she held Martha's hand,
hard, with a fierceness that forced Martha to be
quiet. They must not let the person—if it was a
person—know.

She held hard to Martha's hand until the fear,
which was like a flame, died down. "Let's run,"
Martha whispered, her eyes big. But Adele shook
her head slowly back and forth. They couldn't run
because there was nowhere to go. There were only
the fields surrounding the house, and they couldn't
run into the plowed rows like rabbits.

Adele strained her ears, but the house remained
silent around them. Every time, it was harder to
open the door into that silence. And because the
fear grew worse and worse, she had worked out a
plan. One day soon she would take Martha and
they would go to Grandma and Grandpa's down in
Arkansas. As she stood holding Martha's hand, her
back pressed against the door, Adele knew this
might be the day for them to go. They didn't have

to stay in the house alone, listening for footsteps, watching the light dim in all the rooms.

But then she remembered. The money she'd saved for the trip was upstairs, in their bedroom.

Still holding Martha's hand, Adele tiptoed across the floor, her eyes searching the corners. There was nothing behind the sofa, nothing under the dining-room table. Quickly she looked up the stairs, studying the landing.

There! From the corner of her eye she saw a shadow skim up the staircase.

She drew in her breath and fell back against Martha who grabbed her from behind and held her tight. "What is it? What is it?" Martha said, too scared to be quiet.

Adele looked fully at the stairs and saw there was nothing, not even a shadow. The shadow had only been in the corner of her eye, the way something would slip past when she moved her head quickly.

"Nothing," she told Martha. "I don't think it was anything."

Suddenly she felt braver.

Through the kitchen doorway she could see the sink piled high with dishes, the handle of an iron skillet sticking out.

"We'll need a weapon," she whispered to Martha. "I'm going to get the skillet."

Martha would have run ahead to grab the skillet herself, but Adele held her back. She was older and should be the one to take chances.

It was hard to pull the heavy skillet from the sink. Adele used both hands and yanked, suddenly jerking it free so the dishes clattered. She jumped and looked over her shoulder.

But the noise seemed to please Martha, and she

rattled the dishes again. Now that they had a weapon Martha seemed confident. She ran ahead although Adele called for her to wait. But Martha was naturally braver than she was. It was Martha who flung open the coat closet and kicked the boots into a corner. It was Martha who charged up the stairs dodging the toys, although Adele grabbed her skirt, trying to pull her back.

But at the door of their mother's bedroom they both grew quiet. It was the room Adele feared the most. She felt sure that if something shadowy had moved up the stairs it had taken refuge there.

Adele stepped in front of Martha and slowly opened the door a crack, leaning forward to peer into the room. But it was Martha who suddenly pushed the door wide open so that the bed, the bureaus, the dull light coming through the north windows, were revealed to them both.

While Adele waited in the middle of the floor holding the skillet in her upraised hands, Martha ran through the room to open the closet doors and then lay on the floor on her stomach to look under the bed. "Not in here. Not under there," she called out.

There was no man watching from the back of the closet. There was nothing in the room that could be beaten back with a skillet. And yet Adele was not sure. She still believed that when they came into the house after school they had not been alone. Something had seen them. Something had passed through those rooms.

"Nobody's here, Adele. Can't we stop looking now?" Martha said, brushing spiderwebs from the front of her dress.

"Okay," Adele agreed.

"I was the one that opened all the closets," Martha said. "You were more scared than I was."

If it had been anyone except Martha saying that, Adele would have put her hands on her hips and drawn back her shoulders, standing in that way that her father said made her look like a queen. To anyone except Martha she would have said something smart. But it made her feel bad when she and Martha quarreled because now they only had each other. The others had stopped noticing them.

Now, when she thought about that picture she had in her mind, the one of all of them sitting around the picnic table on the narrow benches, she could see only the middle. The edges were eaten away, the black splotches had spread. She couldn't see the boys, couldn't see the boys at all, and their father was gone too. Just his hand was left, reaching for the salt. That one hand was still caught in the light. It was impossible to tell any longer what expression was on their mother's face, whether or not she was smiling, although in the beginning Adele had been certain she was. She was sure that the next time she thought about the picture her mother would have disappeared, her image eaten away by the blackness. Only she and Martha, sitting on the middle of the bench, in the spot where the sunlight fell through the leaves of the trees— the two of them rolling a jacks ball between their hands and laughing into each other's eyes—would still be in the light.

"We ought to do the dishes, Martha," she told her as they started back down the stairs. "Mother would like that, if we did."

"We could do them later," Martha said. "She won't be back for a long time."

"All right," Adele said, weakening.

There were too many dishes in the sink. Martha would never stick out to help wash and dry them all.

"We could make some peanut-butter sandwiches and take them upstairs," she told Martha. If they made sandwiches and poured glasses of milk to take with them, they wouldn't have to come downstairs again. They would go into their room and shut the door, pushing Martha's desk against it to block anybody trying to get in. With the lamps turned on, their room would be the safest place. Once inside, they would not have to think about the rest of the house as the darkness settled in the rooms. They might feel so safe she would put her plans for leaving out of her mind.

With all three lamps in their room turned on and the desk pushed against the door, Adele stood in front of the mirror and watched as she pulled back her hair, bunching it in one hand and lifting it to the top of her head. Mother wanted to cut her hair and give her a permanent so her hair would be wavy the way Martha's was, but she had decided against this. She liked her hair long and straight because she liked the feel of it on her shoulders, brushing against her cheek when she turned her head quickly. It reminded her of a horse's mane.

Martha was prettier than she was with her deep-blue eyes and short curly hair, but she didn't mind. It wasn't important to her to be pretty or even beautiful. She liked her looks. She liked being thin and brown and quick, and she didn't care if the kids at school did say she looked like a monkey. She was smarter than all the rest of them put together. And what happened at school wasn't important.

"You want to play ranch?" Martha asked. She was already on the floor, squatting on her heels, looking down at the corner where they had it set up. The horses were in their pasture beside the log cabin. The dolls they used to play ranch came of different sets so the girl dolls were as big as the mother and father dolls. But it didn't matter as long as they had a father and a mother and two girls. All the family slept together in the one room of their log cabin, and there was a dog that lived with the family too. In the barn there were several horses, and after breakfast the family fed the horses and took them for long rides through the fields. It seemed to be always summer in the place where the cabin was; the horses could eat grass all year long.

Adele and Martha had played ranch for a long, long time—ever since Adele was five and got the plastic horses for Christmas. The story never changed much. The ranch family did the same things each day, but this was one of the things Adele and Martha liked about the game. They understood the rules perfectly and never had to discuss them. Sometimes Adele took the girl wearing a cowboy hat and made her talk, and sometimes she took the other one, the one with her hair cut short. There was no set way about the mother and father. Whichever one of them felt like moving the parents around did it. The mother and father usually didn't have much to say anyway.

But now sometimes Adele didn't like playing ranch as much as she used to. It was hard for her to keep her mind on the story. But ranch was still

Martha's favorite game, so she squatted on the floor beside her and picked up the girl wearing the cowboy hat.

"It's time for them to get up," she told Martha. "The sun is just coming up and the horses are getting hungry out there in the barn."

Adele had the girl wearing the cowboy hat go into the barn and say hello to the horses snorting in their stalls, waiting for hay to be thrown down to them from the loft. The barn, as Adele saw it, was a lot like Grandpa Trotter's barn in Arkansas, only Grandpa didn't keep horses any longer. Still, she remembered the coolness of the barn and the way the stalls smelled of hay.

When she played this game with Martha everything became very simple. It was like the readers in first grade where everything was set out in big letters. First the family did this and then they did that. It was so soothing her eyelids grew heavy. She could even carry on the game when she was half asleep.

When it was nearly dark she got up to pull the shades down. As she leaned against the glass, letting her eyes sweep over the fields and over the row of trees in the distance, she saw what seemed to be a car or a truck on the dead-end road that ran between the fields. But it was too dark to see clearly, and even if a car did sit there so late in the day it was probably just boys drinking beer.

She pulled the shade down, and the ring on the end of the string rattled against the wall.

"Momma must be working late again," she said to Martha, but Martha was intent on the game and didn't notice.

It was time for the ranch family to brush the

horses' coats with currycombs. This was the last job
of the day, and after that the ranch family would
eat supper. Inside the log cabin it would be the
way it was at Grandma's house when everyone ate
at the wooden table covered with oilcloth. They all
sat so close together their elbows touched as they
lifted the heavy bowls of food and passed them.

While she and Martha were deciding what the
ranch family was going to eat for supper, a sudden
terrible knowledge came to Adele. She would not
tell Martha what she knew, but she was certain that
a storm would come up in the night while the
ranch family slept. While they were asleep—the
mother and the father and the two girls in a row—
the house would cave in on them. They would all
be crushed, even the dog, under the heavy logs.

Adele felt sorry for the ranch family, so soon to
die. "Why don't they have fried chicken and corn-
bread, the kind Grandma makes for us when we go
down there? And buttermilk pie for dessert."

"I don't care," Martha said, and moved the dolls
into the house so they could sit around the table.

Lenora

Every time the phone rang a little shock went down her backbone. She couldn't help it. Seemed like Betty took spite in getting to the phone every time, her voice going all warm and intimate, showing the call was for her and she was much in demand. People from all over with time on their hands had nothing better to do with it than telephone Betty Lederman and yak away. That's what you got to do if the shop belonged to you. Betty could stay on the phone half the afternoon if she wanted to. But heaven help Lenora if *she* spent more than three minutes talking to somebody every once in a while. The black looks Betty cast her way would curl a cat's tail. She knew Betty had suspicions about her private life. But Betty could go fly a kite. Lenora's life wasn't influenced in any way by what Betty Lederman thought or didn't think.

"A little more to the side, maybe?" her customer, old Mrs. Harkins, was saying. "Would that look good on me?"

Nothing would look good on you, honey, was what she thought, but she wouldn't say it. The poor old thing couldn't help how she looked. She might not even be aware of the way her hair had grown so thin on top. Lenora wasn't sharp with the old ones the way Betty got sometimes. They were fussy, the poor old things, and they could give you a hard time, but *she* never forgot what a thin little stick her own mother was before she died. She had feeling for the old.

"I think that might look real good," she told Mrs. Harkins, running her comb carefully down the pink scalp and turning the wisp of hair she managed to pick up onto the other side of the part. "Your hair's just as soft as baby-chick down. Did you know that?"

The poor old thing smiled, showing a row of teeth too even ever to have been real.

We don't ever get too old to want to hear how pretty we look, Lenora thought; and this depressed her and made her count her own years. The good ones she meant, the ones she had left that might benefit her. She had customers who looked good at fifty and even, in some cases, at sixty. They still had some juice in them and a certain gleam in the eye. But they were usually the solid ones—the ones with some flesh, though not too much, to their bones. The kind like her, the thin ones, tended to go quicker. The only thing that might save her was the roundness of her face. Plump skin like that didn't run easily to wrinkles. So she appreciated her face now, though when she was a girl she hadn't liked it much. A kind of cowy look about it she'd always thought, though Burl insisted her face was like a valentine. In the shape of a flower of some kind but he couldn't remember its name.

The telephone rang and she jumped in spite of herself, standing poised with the comb hovering while Betty picked up the receiver. She was sure it was going to be for her, God rewarding her for being kind to old Mrs. Harkins.

But the seconds ticking by after Betty said hello went on too long. So it couldn't be for her after all. And when Betty started talking, her voice getting that excited sound, Lenora felt her heart sink. Gloom, as bad as the cold day, settled over her.

He wasn't going to call. She might as well make up her mind to it. He was tired of her and wouldn't call her again. She would have to learn to live with that the best way she could.

"I'll give you a call sometime Wednesday afternoon if I can, sweetheart." That was what he'd said, the exact words, and at the time she'd just been so happy to have him mention the next time that she hadn't given a thought to what it would mean to wait all Wednesday afternoon, jumping every time the phone rang. And he didn't have to do it that way either. Why couldn't he have said he'd call at three or four? Some definite time. Then she wouldn't have had to go through the awful waiting that kept her half crazy for hours. But it wouldn't enter his head what it was like to be on the other end of that telephone. He'd never been there himself since more than likely he'd always been the one taking charge and making the calls. How would he know how it felt?

Yet she knew—though it cost her to admit it—

that if he cared about her he wouldn't do it this way. She'd better try to face that. He was starting to slide her out the door and ease her out of his life.

She shouldn't have told him about Burl's moving out of the house. That look on Charles's face after she told him hadn't been lost on her. It was just as sure as if he'd taken a big step backwards away from her, only it was just his eyes that did it. Only his eyes took that step away. But how was she supposed to keep a fact like Burl's moving out a secret from him? Somebody just tell her that. Still, she could see now that she should have put off telling Charles as long as possible.

Only—and it was terrible to see how these things came around and slapped you in the face—she had thought Charles would be tickled to hear that Burl had moved out. She thought he'd be pleased to know that now they could get together at her house whenever she could get away from the shop during the day. She'd already made it clear she couldn't have him at the house when Adele and Martha were around, and she didn't want the boys to know either, though it wouldn't surprise her if they guessed.

Another thing she shouldn't have done was tell Burl about Charles. She would have lied up one side and down the other if she had known he'd take it as hard as he did. Not that he was as lily-white innocent as he made out. He'd had a few good-time girls in his time, and if she had to she could name times and places. But for her it was just this one time, just this one thing she wanted. And it wouldn't be but for a while. She'd never supposed it could be any more than that. It was a miracle that Charles had ever wanted her, even for a little while, and it seemed to her that Burl ought to understand. But of course he hadn't. Anybody in his right mind could have told her he wouldn't too. But in some ways she'd been as innocent as a lamb. She hadn't known what love could do to a person.

The thing was, she *couldn't* have said no to Charles. No, not even if she'd known that the very next day she was going to be taken out somewhere and shot. If they'd showed her the gun and set her feet in the place where she was going to have to stand, up against a tree somewhere, it wouldn't have made her do any more than just say, Oh, well, isn't that something interesting now. Nothing, not Burl and not her little girls with their sweet faces, had any power to stop her. Not God Himself unless He'd struck her dead on the spot.

It was a terrible thing to be driven like that—it wasn't that she didn't know it. And still she'd never been as happy in her life. It was a state that nothing had prepared her for. Not her upbringing or what her mother had told her about what was right or wrong, and not anything either that had ever been said in Sunday school when she was growing up.

The closest thing to her own state she knew of in the Bible was the way King David had fallen for Bathsheba when he saw her taking that bath on the roof in the cool of the day and knew on the instant he had to have her for himself no matter what the cost. What she would never have understood from what was said about the story in Baptist Sunday school was how David couldn't help it. Once he saw Bathsheba up on that roof, nothing else in the world mattered to him. Other questions didn't

enter in. She'd never had any particular sympathy
for David before, but now she had to see the story
in a new light. Oh, Charles, Charles! She didn't
care what else, if only he would call. Wrongdoing
or whatever anybody might say about it. She
couldn't give that a thought. If he would just telephone and want to see her again.

Suddenly her hands went slick. The comb
slipped right out of her hand and fell to the floor.
Old Mrs. Harkins, nearly combed out, craned her
head around to see. "Butterfingers this afternoon,
aren't you?" she said, smiling her careful smile
around all those teeth. But Lenora couldn't pay
attention, not even to make a remark.

She'd forgotten, but of a sudden it came back to
her—just *how* it was God had gotten back at David.
That poor little boy baby he and Bathsheba had,
taken by God in some sickness. And there were her
own two little girls stuck in that house in the middle of those empty fields, an invitation for any kind
of pervert. The night was falling too, and by the
time she got home it would be as dark as the inside
of a pocket.

She gave a final little puff to the hair that framed
Mrs. Harkins's face, and turned the chair around
so she could take a look at the back. Of course Mrs.
Harkins seemed to take forever, holding up the
mirror with a shaky hand that looked a lot like a
claw, patting her waves on each side, puffing up the
top, turning her head from side to side like a bird.
Then she was untying Mrs. Harkins from the protective bib and helping her to her feet. Betty
would take the money if she could get her over to
the desk. All she'd have to do then was put away
the curlers and setting lotion. It wouldn't take long

since it was Betty's turn to sweep up and empty the solutions for the permanents. In five minutes she'd be through. But she was just sweeping the curlers into the drawer when Betty's voice caught her and held her where she was.

"Could you be sweet and clean up for me today, Lenora? I've got to get to the post office before it closes, and I'll just make it if I run now."

It was on her tongue to say that she'd cleaned up for the last two days and she had to get on home herself. But she caught the words where they were and held them back. Betty could do what she liked, but she couldn't. This was the only job she had and she didn't see how, even with it, she would ever be able to pay the rent now that it looked like she was stuck with the whole thing. And if she started explaining to Betty why she needed to get home, there was no telling where it would end. One thing she didn't want was Betty shoving her nose into her private life.

So of course she had to say yes. She'd do it. She'd clean up and lock the place.

There was the floor to sweep, the counters to wipe off, the dirty towels to put in the bag. She was in the back room emptying the permanent-wave solution into the sink—the last thing, she was nearly ready to run for the door, when the telephone rang. That first moment, so help her God, she didn't even think about Charles. She just thought, Now who the heck could that be, calling after closing time when there's not supposed to be anybody here?

So when she heard Charles's voice on the other end of the line she couldn't believe it. A rush of such pleasure came to her head that for a minute she thought she might faint.

"I was just about to go out the door. Five minutes more and I'd have been gone. I'd just about given you out, as they say down home."

"I've been so busy all afternoon you wouldn't believe it. One customer right after another without a letup."

She was so glad to hear his voice, to know he'd *wanted* to call her, that she could have burst into song right there.

"I was just ready to run out the door," she told him. "Another minute and you wouldn't have caught me." She knew she oughtn't to rattle on to him like that, but she was too happy and relieved to keep quiet.

"I was wondering about tonight," he said. "Any chance of us getting together?"

Her heart began gathering speed, and she had to open her mouth to breathe since she felt she knew what he was going to say next, before he even voiced the words.

"I was just thinking maybe if I came over to your place late tonight. After your little girls are asleep. How would that be?"

"Could you get out then?"

"I've told you how I wander around the house most of the night. Sometimes I go for long walks. So Sylvia wouldn't think anything of it if she woke up and I wasn't there."

"I sure want to see you, Charles," she started out, wondering how she ought to proceed. But it wasn't her choice to have him come to her house at night like that. The daytime was all right. She couldn't see anything wrong with that. If the neighbors noticed anything—well, let them. Since she was just a renter and they didn't take her seriously, why should they care what she did or didn't do? But this other way, this coming at night, didn't set too well with her. The boys slept in that place they'd fixed up for themselves above the garage, and might not notice. Or if they did they probably wouldn't care. But then there were the girls.

"What if the girls woke up in the night and came looking for me?" she said to Charles. "That sure wouldn't look very good, would it, their mother in bed with somebody they'd never set eyes on before?"

"If you don't want to . . ." he said, and she knew it as well as if she could see his face—something in his eyes going distant.

"You know I want to," she said quickly. And she did. A little quivering had started up in her stomach, and her legs were beginning to go weak. Truth to tell, she wanted to be with him so much she couldn't stand it. She wished there was some way she could come right out and say how much she wanted to see him. But she couldn't bring herself to. The words wouldn't come past her lips.

"Well, I don't know where else you think we might go," he said, and she could still hear that little distance in his voice. "It's cold for the backseat of a car, wouldn't you say? And can you see us going to the Holiday Inn in the middle of the night, in this town? So there isn't but one way I know and if you say that's out . . ."

"Look. I guess it'll be all right," she said, giving in quickly before he got fed up with her and decided it was all too much trouble. "I don't know what I'm so worried about. I can't even remember the last time either one of the girls got up in the night. Only if they were sick or something. So let's just plan on doing it. What time do you think you'll come?"

There it was again. That little drawing back. That unwillingness to be put on the spot.

"Listen, Lenora, I can't give you the exact time and minute, can I? Just think about it. Depends on what time Sylvia goes to bed. Depends on when I *can*. Oh, late. Has to be late. Sometime in the early morning."

So it was going to be another of those times—she knew it. Her night of sleep would be ruined. She would be like a person under sentence of death waiting for a pardon at the last minute. But it didn't matter, she didn't care. Oh, she was just happy because he was going to come. She should be the most grateful woman on earth that he would leave his warm house in the middle of the night and drive five miles into the country just to be with her for an hour. It was a miracle that he would be willing to do all that for her. So the waiting wouldn't matter as long as she knew for sure he was going to come. The waiting could even be the sweetest, most thrilling thing. It would give her time to get ready for him and be all prepared so when he did come they wouldn't have to waste a minute. He was going to come! It was all arranged and the only thing she had to do was wait.

"You just come on as soon as you can," she told him. "You know I'll be waiting."

"See you later, then," he said, and eased the receiver onto the cradle.

She could have danced out the door, could have

shouted to the world. She didn't even notice the cold when she shut the door behind her, and the fact that it was dark outside didn't distress her either.

It wasn't until she was already halfway home that the thought of the girls came to her again, and when it did she didn't get upset. Her fear for them had just been some idea she'd gotten because she was worried sick about Charles's not telephoning. This wasn't the kind of place where perverts hung out. There wasn't anything to be afraid of in the country. People went to bed at a decent hour and didn't get into trouble that she knew about.

So she was sure, just as sure as she knew anything, that the girls were all right. Her mother instinct told her that. She would be bound to know, for sure, if anything bad had happened. But it hadn't. It wouldn't. God didn't pay as much attention to what went on down here as He once had. King David just had the misfortune to live in a time when God bothered more. By now He'd probably given up on the whole thing.

Burl

WHEN Burl opened his eyes on darkness, he groped like a blind person, frantic to know where he was. Only after he knocked his hand against the steering wheel of the truck did he remember. "Son of a bitch," he said, stiffly pulling himself upright on the seat. As soon as he sat up the cold got to him, and he started shivering. In front of him there was the shape of the truck hood and beyond it some dim, bare trees. Somewhere out there a small pinpoint of light burned.

The last thing he remembered was sliding down on the slick seat of the truck with his knees doubled against his chest and his hands in his pockets, planning to rest a few minutes. He had time to spare and nothing whatever to do with it. Whole thing reminded him strongly of waiting around at a deer or turkey blind, sitting there hunkered on his heels waiting for something to show up. Lying in wait for a deer or for a man was the same thing. Both meant a lot of hanging around and wishing he had a bottle of Jack Daniel's to warm him up.

He hadn't intended to go to sleep, but now it seemed the best thing he could have done. Time passed quickly when you were asleep, and the only bad thing was waking up cold, and stiff as a piece of wood.

Burl figured that the light he could see, wavering when a tree branch blew in front of it, was the light from the girls' bedroom. Adele and Martha, his little girls, all by themselves up there in the top of the house. The rest of the place was dark as a hole. So it must seem to them they were the last people left on earth.

But, strictly speaking, they weren't alone. There he was, after all, keeping an eye on them, watching them just like God, although he guessed God could see through the roof and the walls too in a way Burl was not privileged to do.

It made him feel good to watch over his girls even though they couldn't know he was out there doing it. But he bet they'd be tickled to know their daddy was sitting not half a mile from the house, watching the light coming from their bedroom window. They'd probably laugh if they could see him slapping his hands against his ribs and beating his thighs together trying to get up his circulation. He'd always been a good daddy to his girls, reading them the funny papers when they were little things climbing into his lap, calling out to them first thing when he came into the house in the evenings. He knew they were lonesome without him. They probably asked every day when he was coming back home.

It made him want to cry every time he thought about his poor little girls, wondering where their daddy was. Forced out of his own house by that haircutter. He was the one without even a home anymore, though not any part of it had been his fault.

"It's not fair!" he shouted into the darkness. "You hear me?"

It was the sight of the house, suddenly bursting into bloom with light, that jarred him into action, so he suddenly stretched his legs and turned the key in the ignition. Movement, the knowledge that events were moving forward, cheered him up considerably.

As soon as the motor turned over he flicked on the radio which he kept set for WOKQ. If it wasn't news coming on, it would be some music worth listening to. And there it came, loud and clear, Kenny Rogers singing "Let's Go Out in a Blaze of Glory." He sang along, filling the cab with sound. He was going to go out in a blaze of glory himself, taking Lenora and the haircutter with him. The thought made him happy.

There wasn't a chance, since it was so dark, that Lenora could make out his truck driving past her front windows, so as he drove by he slowed down and looked close. She hadn't pulled the shades— which was just like Lenora—so he got a good look as he passed by. Anybody else could have looked in and seen too, but Lenora had never been one for taking precautions.

There she was just standing in the middle of the kitchen, not doing, so far as he could make out, one thing. Her head, he noticed, was on one side, the way she held it when she was thinking. Not many knew but he did—lord, he'd lived with Lenora for going on twenty years—that one of her eyes was set higher in her head than the other one. She saw the world crooked. But she was too vain to wear glasses, which she ought to have done, so what she had to do was hold her head on one side to make things she was looking at come out even. Lenora wasn't worth a damn hanging pictures.

It made him feel bad to see her standing in that way he knew so well. It made him feel like pulling into the driveway and walking on into the house, asking what was for supper. If he did that, what did he suppose would happen? His welcome wouldn't be exactly overwhelming; he guessed that. And he was too mad at Lenora to try to pull that off anyway. It was only a thought in passing.

He went on slowly past the driveway, making sure hers was the only car in it. Which it was, but he'd expected this. Since the haircutter hadn't come earlier in the afternoon, then he wouldn't be over until late. That was clear. But Burl didn't intend to leave any possibility unchecked. Having come this far, he wasn't about to take even one chance that would let the haircutter slip through his fingers. But once he saw that Lenora's was the only car in the driveway, he figured it would be all right to go off for a little while to eat and warm up. He'd be back. He had all the time in the world.

Lenora

SHE hadn't any more than turned the handle of the door when she heard Adele calling out from the top of the stairs, her voice quivery the way it had been when she was little. It hurt Lenora to hear that note in her child's voice. Of course Adele and Martha were scared in that big old house after dark, with just the two of them rattling around in it. She'd known all along they were scared, but what could she do? There wasn't anybody who could be home when the girls got off the school bus—that was just a cruel fact of life.

"I'm home!" she called out. "Precious babies!"

She felt such a rush of love for them as they came running down the stairs. Martha got to her first. Lenora noted that in every family she'd ever known, the youngest was like that. The youngest was a loving child.

Oh, but Adele loved her too. She knew Adele loved her just as dearly as Martha, but Adele was more backward in showing it. She'd always been like that, waiting for somebody else to make the first move.

But she loved her girls equally. She loved her boys too, but her boys had grown past her. So would the girls. But then, not altogether. Not for good. Girls came back to their folks after they'd gotten the wildness out of their systems. But boys were gone for good. It had been like that with her brothers, so she knew what to expect. She was always glad to see them when she went down home, but after fifteen minutes of asking about the crops and what kind of a year they'd had, what was there to say? It wasn't like that with her sisters, though. With them she could talk a mile a minute and never get it all said. They had all stayed close, even as grown-up women. So she was sure the love she poured out on the girls wouldn't be wasted. It would be returned to her many times over.

"You poor little things," she told them. "Here all by yourselves. Bet you were scared, weren't you?"

"Adele thought somebody was in the house when we came in," Martha told her. "We had to go through every room with a skillet. Wasn't anybody, though."

"Oh, I'll bet you were scared," Lenora said, drawing Adele over to her and making sure she got a hug. "But who'd want to come in this house? The mess in this room right here would scare off any bugger."

Martha thought that was funny, but Adele wouldn't crack a smile. It was hard to hit it just right with Adele, but it was easy for Lenora to know what would make Martha laugh. Martha was

more like her—was *just* like her, to tell the truth—
even taking after her in looks.

"Couldn't you girls have done a little bit of
cleaning up around here when you came in from
school? Didn't do anything but play, did you?
Never noticed what a mess everything was in."

If she hadn't felt bad about being forced to leave
the girls in the house so much by themselves, she
would've gotten angrier. As it was, it didn't seem
right to blame them. They were just children. But
they didn't have any idea what it was like for her,
coming home after being on her feet all day long,
with supper to get on the table, and everything in
this state. Somehow, with Burl leaving the way he
had, she had lost heart about the house. It was too
much, her burden was too great, and not even
Charles's love could ease it altogether.

She sent the girls to get the big trash can from
the backyard so she could start them on the living
room. They could throw away all those beer cans
that lined the windowsills, for a start. Blame the
boys for the cans. Everywhere she turned there was
some job needing doing, and for a minute she just
stood beside the kitchen table, too tired to move.

The whole place was going to have to be cleaned
up before Charles got there. It would make a terrible impression if he saw that mess. Other times,
when he'd come in the daytime, she'd led him from
the back door directly up the stairs, and he hadn't
seen much except the bedroom. But this time there
was no telling which door he might come in. And
even before she could get supper on the table,
there was that sink full of dishes. Most of them
could be laid directly at Jeff and Scott's feet too,
but no use expecting them to do their share of the

work because they wouldn't. They didn't consider that they were living with her any longer, so why should they help out? It didn't escape her notice, though, that they weren't above eating the food she brought in. But then, of course they were still her sons, and she'd take what responsibility she could. *Burl* seemed to have slipped that harness mighty easy, which was the way men were. Here she had the rent, the electricity and oil—everything hanging over her head. And besides that, there were the girls to take care of and the boys expecting her to cook for them. But Burl just ran off in a huff, glad to dump everything in her lap.

She raised her head all of a sudden and looked at the black expanse of glass where the windows were. Somebody was out there looking in; she could just swear it. She leaned forward trying to see, but there was nothing visible except her own self looking startled as a deer, caught in all that black.

Angrily she grabbed the bottoms of the shades and yanked them all the way down. *Now* let somebody just try to look in. They wouldn't see much.

Adele

Even before she came downstairs, when she was standing behind the railing, calling down to who-ever had opened the door, Adele heard that false note in her mother's voice. The sound could be taken as loving—*babies,* the voice said, *precious babies*—but it was hollow where it should have been full and rich. Before, when their mother had really loved them, her voice had been like cream, heavy on her tongue. But now there was something thin and anxious in it. She said the right words, but they were like shadows.

Yet it *was* her mother standing in the doorway— the slender woman with the halo of golden hair around her head. Her mother had hair like Martha's; but there were lines of tiredness in her face, and her brown coat, pulled down on one shoulder and tied crookedly with a belt, would let the cold get in. Of course it was her mother, no one else, but the mother she knew was not there inside the eyes that failed to see Martha or her standing there even while she smiled. Or even while she held out her arms to love them. Her arms touched Adele's shoulders like sticks.

So Adele held back and didn't go to her. It was scary to know they could not rely on their mother either, now that their father had moved out of the house. And the boys had seen what was coming before she did. Only she and Martha were left alone while the darkness came up from the fields and blotted away everything outside the house.

When Scott and Jeff had been younger they had let her play with them sometimes. They had been big brothers who could give rides on their backs, and she had looked up to them and thought they were very wise. But now that they had moved out of the house it hardly seemed they were part of the family anymore. She missed seeing them every day the way it had been before. Yet they were just across the driveway, no distance at all, and there was no reason she shouldn't tell them about the way it was, coming into the house every afternoon, or about the shadow she'd seen moving up the stairs.

When she and Martha went outside to bring in the trash can the way their mother told them, she could feel the air heavy the way it was before a storm. Above their heads there was only blackness. Not a star shone. Maybe this was the reason she felt edgy. It was just a storm moving in over the lake. When they were working on the house in the summer, she remembered how their father had pointed to the north with the hammer he held in his hand. "That's the way the storms will blow in on us in the winter. Right off the lake. But when we put up the storm windows and seal them up, we'll stay as warm as Florida."

She and Martha pulled the trash can into the living room and started on the beer cans. That was easy. She liked to smash the cans in her hands and watch the pale-brown liquid bubble out the top. Once her father had held out a can of beer to her for a taste, and she'd touched her tongue to the slot in the top. She'd drawn back quickly, though, because the beer had a sharp, bitter taste. Her father had laughed at the face she made.

In the kitchen she set the knives, forks, and spoons on the table, and Martha put out the plates.

"You want me to put out six plates?" Martha asked, but their mother shook her head as though the question got on her nerves. Martha asked the same thing every night because she hadn't understood that their father wasn't going to eat with them again. Adele never set a place for him. She knew he wasn't coming back because she had heard the shouting in the nights. But Martha had slept through all the fights so she could never remember about their father.

Their mother and father had fought other times too, but those fights hadn't been important. There was the time their mother was so angry she set a bowl of beans down in the middle of the table, hard, and the bowl had cracked. There was another time when their father drove the car, with all of them in it, straight into a ditch and sat with his arms folded over his chest, not moving until their mother took back something she'd said. She and Martha and Scott and Jeff had laughed at these fights.

But the shouting in the night at the farmhouse was different—it was mean and dangerous. It wasn't so much the words—which she couldn't always hear —but what lay under them. A sound that meant they hated each other.

"You think it's going to snow?" Adele asked as she placed the knives beside the plates. "I think maybe it's going to snow."

"Oh, I don't think it's cold enough. It's not but November, Adele. You want it to snow so you can go on your sled?"

"I think it's going to storm, maybe."

"The air's just as still. You don't have to worry about any storm coming up tonight."

She watched her mother spread fish sticks over the surface of a cookie sheet, spreading them out so they wouldn't touch each other.

"We had fish sticks last night," Martha said.

"Honey, I know it. But I'm just so tired when I get in from work. I can't cook up a lot of stuff. And you like fish sticks anyway. Don't you?"

"They're okay. I don't care."

Their mother was smaller than Grandma was. Mother was thin and her wrists were so small the bones reminded Adele of a chicken's wishbone. When she was very little she'd sat in her mother's lap scooting around, trying to find a comfortable place, but her mother's legs were bony and when she leaned back against her chest, that was bony too. Grandma's lap was cushiony and her hands smelled like flour. Adele could remember holding her grandmother's hands up to her nose.

"There was somebody in the house when we came in after school," Adele said, carrying two glasses of milk to the table.

"Aw, there wasn't," Martha said. "We looked all around and there wasn't anybody here, Adele. You know there wasn't."

"He just went out the back door, is all. I knew it all along, only I didn't want to scare you. I knew he was in here as soon as I opened the door."

"The door was locked, wasn't it?" their mother asked. "I always lock it and I've told you over and over, Adele—"

"He was here. I even saw him move in the hallway by the back door." Something stubborn made her insist on that, even though she knew there hadn't been any man in the house. She had seen the shadow, though, gliding up the stairs.

"Did you really?" Martha said. "I didn't see anybody."

"I don't tell you *everything*."

"You know what happens to little girls who tell stories," their mother said.

"The house is so dark and scary when we come home after school."

Her mother looked at Adele, a thin line suddenly slanting across her forehead as it did when she was getting angry. "Well, just what do you want me to do about it, Adele, you answer me that? You want me to quit work so we'll all go hungry and won't have a house to live in? You want us to live out in the fields like wild animals or something? Because for your information, if you want the truth, I don't even know where the rent money's going to come from this month. Your daddy didn't give a thought to that before he ran off, did he? And where does that leave us now? I am just so tired I could sit down right here and cry, so if you want to see your momma cry you just go on telling stories about coming in a scary house every afternoon because there isn't one thing I can do about it."

Adele watched her mother snap shut the oven door with a bang and saw in her eyes that she wanted to leave too, as their father had. It was there, plain. Distance wide as a field.

"You better just sit down at that table and be good, now, because I could say a thing or two about the way you girls come in this house and never turn your hands, even though jobs are crying out to be done. When I wasn't but Martha's age I had all the dish washing to do by myself and that wasn't all I did either."

Adele stopped listening to the words and heard only the flow of her mother's voice. She wished she hadn't said anything about how it was coming into the house in the afternoons, after all. She knew her mother couldn't do anything about it.

"You want me to go get the boys?" she asked. "I don't mind going over there."

Before her mother answered, Adele grabbed her coat and ran out, wanting to go before Martha made up her mind to come too.

The light was on in the room above the garage, so she knew the boys were there. The wooden stairs rattled under her feet as she ran up, and so she thought the boys would hear and didn't knock even though Scott had bawled her out more than once for coming into their place without warning. She knew they smoked pot up there. Everybody, even their mother, knew that, and she knew they brought girls up there too, girls who would spend the night with them. She had looked out the window early in the morning and had seen girls com-

ing down the stairs, holding the railing and moving slowly as though they were afraid they might
slip. There was one girl she even recognized from
riding the school bus, a girl named Marilyn or
Mary Lynn. But she hadn't shown she knew, had
never so much as looked hard in the girl's direction, when they rode the bus together. Though
once, when their eyes happened to catch, she
thought the girl had winked at her.

Tonight she didn't think there was anybody
with the boys, but still, when she pushed open the
door and came into the room, she felt a little shy. It
was cold in the boys' room because they hadn't
much more than gotten the stove going. They were
still in their jackets and had beers already opened.

Both Scott and Jeff were wearing black leather
jackets—the kind people wear to ride motorcycles
—and black boots with rounded, stubby toes. Both
of them wore their hair slicked back straight from
their foreheads, and this made them look older
than they were and also made them appear to look
alike, even though Scott was heavier and broader
through the shoulders than Jeff was.

Those times she saw Scott and Jeff she tended to
look at them more closely than she did at Martha
because she saw Martha every day. She slept with
Martha and got up with Martha. But whole days
went by when she didn't see the boys. It hadn't
always been like that. Only a short time before, the
boys had littered the house with their footballs and
baseball gloves and filled the house with music
from R.E.O. Speedwagon and Doors records. And a
long time before that, she and Jeff and Scott had
played together. There was the time they made a
house out of a packing crate and played in it for a

long time, for days, and there were other times
when they had pushed toy cars around and around
a tree, working in and out of the roots. They'd
done that many times, many days, maybe a whole
summer. She couldn't remember. But now the boys
were changed. They were grown-up and didn't
even look the way they used to. Then, they had
just been her brothers that she played with, squatting in the dirt with her shoulders touching theirs.
But now they were the same as strangers.

Scott and Jeff both looked at her, though neither
smiled or looked glad to see her. As far as she could
tell, they might never have set eyes on her before.
But it wasn't that they hated her or even disliked
her. It was only that she was different from them,
and they didn't have any place in their lives for a
sister. Not for a sister who was only eleven, at least.
Maybe if she'd been older.

Yet their blood was the same as hers. She could
see how Scott had their father's broad shoulders,
how his nose turned up as their father's did, and
how Jeff and she had their mother's delicate bones.

"Momma said to tell you-all that supper's ready."

She didn't come very far into the room and she
looked at Jeff when she spoke. Though Jeff didn't
talk as much as Scott did—Jeff didn't talk very
much at all—he didn't get angry in the way Scott
did, either. Or if Jeff got mad he didn't show it. It
was hard to tell when Jeff was angry. But Scott
would bawl you out when he felt like it. His face
would go red, and he would make his hands into
fists as though he might be thinking of hitting you
with them. Jeff seemed safer.

"Tell us what supper is," Scott said, "before we
can decide if we want to eat it or not."

"Fish sticks. That and potatoes."

"Again? She fixing that again? That's the very same thing we had to eat last night. Can't she think of anything different?"

"She hadn't got time to fix up a big supper. She's been working since early morning."

"Well, she's not the only one, is she? What'd you think we do all day? Sit around on our hands? Anybody doesn't think we put in a full day had better come follow us around. Just see."

Jeff looked at the wall, cupping his fingers over the top of his beer can. Adele could tell he wasn't going to say anything. Jeff was just going to stand there, not seeing the wall even though his eyes were fixed on it, just standing as though he was run by some kind of motor that had gotten turned off.

"Well, are you going to come eat, or what?"

"Naw. We'll go get ourselves a pizza after a while. There's a limit to how many fish sticks a person can eat."

Scott lifted his can of beer and took a big swallow, keeping his eyes on her but not paying any attention, just waiting for her to turn away with the answer.

There were some tabs, like little silver tongues, pulled from cans of beer and dropped over the floor. She picked up a couple of these and shook them in her closed hand, listening to the faint jingling noise they made.

"I think maybe Martha and me should leave," she told them finally, tossing the silver tabs in her hand. "We ought to go stay with Grandma and Grandpa for a while maybe."

Scott laughed, his lips drawn back over his teeth.

"You can't go running off to Arkansas just like that. You know how far it is?"

She couldn't tell him about the shadow in the house, or about the picture of them all she held in her mind, the picture that was slowly disappearing in the darkness. Scott would just drink his beer, shaking his head and grinning to show that he thought it was all made-up kid stuff you didn't have to pay attention to. And whatever Jeff thought nobody would know because Jeff wouldn't say anything. He might look at her, fixing his eyes on her face instead of the wall, but he wouldn't say anything to show what he was thinking.

"We ought to go, anyway," she said stubbornly, even though as soon as she said the words she wasn't so sure that it was Grandma's where they should go after all. She'd decided on Grandma's because that was the place most like the ranch, the place that seemed the safest. But now she wasn't sure. Maybe she and Martha should go someplace else, a place she hadn't thought of yet. Only she knew Grandma and Grandpa's house so well. She knew what the ground smelled like when you crawled under the front steps—an odd smell like toadstools; and she knew a particular place in the wall where you could stick your finger all the way in and not feel anything at the bottom. She knew many, many other things about that place that showed she hadn't made it up, that it existed and would go on standing—the house and every fence and tree around it—even if she wasn't there to see it.

"Why do you want to go?" Jeff said suddenly. He had a soft voice, one that could easily be drowned out, although when Jeff said something people usually listened.

His face was turned toward her, his eyes following wherever she moved.

"When we came home from school this afternoon there was somebody in the house. I know there was. I could feel him watching us."

"You *saw* somebody?" Scott said.

"His shadow, maybe, in the hallway. I don't know. It was just *something*. Like a shadow. You weren't there, either one of you, so you don't know."

"Like a shadow?" Jeff said, fixing her with eyes of such a pale blue that it didn't seem they would be capable of holding shadows. "Were you scared?"

"It was scary. You would've been scared too."

"But not a face? Just a shape?" Jeff said, watching her.

"I don't know what it was," she said, turning sullen then. The shadow hadn't been important. She'd just said a shadow because that was something they could understand. Just the same way they could understand if she said *a person. A person was in the house.* But it hadn't been a person, and not even a shadow.

"Just kind of hovering there?" Jeff said, looking at her so intently it made her feel embarrassed.

"It might have been hovering," she told him without looking into his face. "Something dark. That's all I know."

"You were just spooked," Scott said. "You were scared coming in the house by yourself."

"I got to go back," she told them.

All the way to the door she could feel Jeff's eyes

on her. Jeff never talked much, but she believed he understood things he never tried to say. Still, you couldn't tell with Jeff. He just stood there, holding the can of beer in his hand, watching her walk to the door.

Jeff

WHAT she saw, what Adele his sister saw, standing in the hallway of the house like a shadow but keeping its head turned away was what he had been expecting. He'd felt her presence near. The angel of death. The shadow Adele had seen was the black sweep of the angel's wings. Jeff was sure of this, though he had not seen the angel clearly himself. Not her shadow or her face, which only those chosen to go with her were privileged to see close up. But the results of her passing he had studied, and he knew that her face was sweet, was of a sweetness that surpassed human understanding. He wanted to ask Adele for every detail of what she had seen. Yet he kept quiet because he didn't want anyone to know how intense his interest was. Nobody knew about his collection of photographs. No one knew how much he pondered the mystery.

In his collection there were many different faces —both old and young, men and women—but he had taken note that all the faces bore a strong resemblance to one another and this had nothing to do with family likeness, even though most of the photographs in his collection were those of his kin.

He'd found the photographs when he was visiting Grandma Trotter the summer he was seven. One hot afternoon when everybody had been taking a nap he had wandered through the house opening the drawers of bureaus and sifting through the contents. Nothing had held his attention for long until he discovered the family photographs lying loose and jumbled in the sideboard in the dining room. At first he had shuffled through them quickly as though there was a particular face he was looking for. But none of those people looking into the eye of the camera held his attention. It was a face in repose—the eyes shut, the mouth set in a faint smile—that he studied for a long time. As he looked through the photographs he found other faces with that same mysterious smile, and to these he returned again and again secretly when no one else was around, sliding open the drawer of the sideboard and taking his favorites into a corner where he could study them in private.

He studied the photographs the same way he studied certain pictures in the family Bible that Grandma kept on a table in the living room. It was such a heavy Bible that he could not lift it to the floor but had to stand on tiptoe to see, turning the pages until he found the picture that showed a mountaintop surrounded by water. Clinging to this one place of safety were many people, holding tightly to one another. In the center of the picture a mother held her baby in her arms, lifting it high. But there was nowhere for the baby or the mother to go. Above the people there was only the heavy sky pouring rain. Everybody in the picture looked terrified. Their mouths were open and their eyes were wild. Jeff knew they were about to drown and that there was no way out of it. His grandmother had told him the story. It made his breath draw tight to see how wild with fear the people looked. Those people were going to die any minute and they knew it. But they didn't look at all like the people in his photographs. Those people didn't look sorry to die. They looked joyful.

The other picture in the Bible that he turned to often was the one of Jesus walking in the garden after he had risen from the dead. Jesus looked more like the people in the photographs. Jesus seemed to glow as though there were a candle burning inside him—the way flame glows through wax. Luminous. Jeff looked back and forth between these pictures, trying to understand their mystery.

Once, in an offhand way, as though it was a question that held little interest for him, he asked his grandmother about one of the photographs.

It was the picture of a little dead baby, she told him. Her own sister's baby that would have grown up to be his second cousin if it had lived.

"But the angel of death passed right over that little baby's cradle and took it off to Jesus," his grandmother told him. "That's why it has such a sweet look on its face."

"Because it's dead?"

His grandmother looked taken aback. "Not because it's *dead,* Jeffy, but because it's gone to Jesus."

"But you can't go to Jesus if you aren't dead, can you?"

His grandmother gave him a worried look.

"Well, no, I guess you can't. But that's not something a little boy should think about. Why don't you go on outside now and play? You oughtn't to be in here when the sun's so bright."

He had known, somehow, even before he asked his grandmother about the baby, that grown-ups didn't like to talk about death. But he'd known, even when he was seven, that what happened when a person passed under the wings of the angel was the most important mystery there was, and that he would have to figure it out for himself.

The images in the photographs were as clear as mountains and trees seen on a bright day when the air was fresh. Every detail stood out. For a long time he looked at the picture of the dead baby, and everything about the picture was so sharp and clear that it seemed he ought to be able to feel the fancywork on its gown—to touch the flowers and leaves. The baby was propped on a pillow and was wearing a long gown that reached to the edge of the picture, and on its head was a bonnet that fluted around its face. The baby, though not unhappy-looking, had a shriveled, hungry look about it. In his opinion the baby looked hungry because it hadn't had time to learn about the place it was passing so briefly through. Since it had gone so quickly from one world to another, catching only a little flash of green in between, it was not surprising that the baby had that unsatisfied look around its lips.

Aside from the baby, there was one other face in his collection that looked less than pleased to pass under the angel's wings. That was his great-grandfather. The photograph showed him laid out in a pine box with the lid taken off for the occasion of the picture taking, lying straight and neat and wearing a fresh white shirt open at the collar. His hands, with fingers interlaced, were resting comfortably on his stomach. Yet the look on his face, caught forever before the lid of the box was lifted into place, was stern and unyielding. Right up to the end he had held on to whatever had kept him going through a long life, and had not relinquished it even to the angel of death. He had looked right back at her, eye to eye, not giving an inch.

But the expression that Jeff liked to see best—the one that drew him again and again—was joyful, even beatific. His very favorite was the photograph of his Aunt Linnie, Grandpa's sister, who had died of brain fever at sixteen. The picture had been taken not more than ten minutes after Linnie breathed her last. There she was, lying with her head on the pillow, the sheet drawn back to her waist and folded neatly. More than once Jeff had heard the story from Grandpa, of how the traveling photographer came to the door and knocked and they all thought he was the preacher who had been sent for. But when they opened the door and saw the photographer standing on the stoop with his camera in a heavy black bag, they realized he was heaven-sent. Linnie had died such a peaceful, Christian death that it still showed clearly in her face. Her eyes, which were closed, seemed nevertheless to be straining to see something that still hovered just above her bed. She was smiling as though whatever it was she was seeing beyond the thin skin of her earthly body was sweet beyond all expression. Her lips had parted, just getting ready to tell them what she was seeing, but she'd never said a word.

What was she trying to tell? This was what drew Jeff again and again to the photographs as he slid the drawer open silently and spread his favorites over the floor. When they left Arkansas that summer he took the photographs with him, telling nobody about them.

The time had passed when he could ask even his grandmother anything more about the angel of death or about what the eyes of the dying saw when it was past the time for words. He would come to his own conclusions.

The more he thought about the angel of death, the clearer her face came to him. That she was beautiful went without saying. Her face as he imagined it was of such perfection that he caught his breath at its purity. But it was her eyes that held him. Looking into those eyes he would know the limits of light, since he knew it wasn't darkness but light that closed the eyes of all the people in his collection and brought that look of joy to their lips. But no matter how closely he looked, no matter how patiently he waited, he could glimpse no more than a shadow of what those others had seen with such wonderful clarity.

He kept the photographs in the back of the Bible his grandmother gave him when he was nine. She gave Scott and Adele and Martha Bibles too, but the others never read theirs as far as he knew. He did read his, though, liking the little flutter as he turned the pages, so thin they were almost transparent. He kept his Bible in the back of his underwear drawer, hiding his collection from the others. Yet even if Scott had found the photographs it wouldn't have mattered. None of them would have understood why the photographs were important, as they failed to understand so many other things.

Scott and Jeff, Jeff and Scott. That was all the rest of the family knew—lumping the two of them together as though they were just the same, as though they were not two people at all but just parts of the same one. Sometimes he hated this, but he had chosen it too. When the others looked at Scott, they could see Jeff only in their side vision, never in focus. So he was left in peace, and nobody interfered with him. They wouldn't have known how. Like a movie of a person shown on a screen, he was always a little too much in the light or too much in the shadow so anybody looking would say later, "Did you notice that person standing over by the tree? Or was that just a shadow? Maybe it was just the leaves moving in the wind."

When he was with people, either at home or at the garage where he worked with Scott, he tried to say what it was the others expected him to say. He moved as this person that they saw so imperfectly moved. He was Jeff, with a particular kind of nose, particular hair. But inside his head he was something else entirely. Inside he was not Jeff, not the one the others thought they knew. Inside his head he had no name.

Burl

THE first matter of importance was to get himself a bottle of whiskey, something to help him fight the cold. He weighed the possibility of buying two bottles—it might be a long night—but decided against getting more than one. If he got himself drunk out there in the yard before that haircutter put in his appearance, then what good was that going to do? If he threw open the door of the bedroom, lifted his gun out of his pocket, and slid right down to the floor drunk as a goat, wouldn't that be a joke? So he confined himself to one bottle and figured he'd better go easy on it.

He knew he might as well fortify himself with food too while he was at it. So after he had bought a bottle of Jack Daniel's, he stood outside the liquor store making up his mind whether he should go to McDonald's or to Friendly's. Friendly's, he figured, might be a better place to sit around awhile so he walked in that direction, feeling the gun bumping into his thigh where it rode in the pocket of his jacket. It was good having it there, a little bit of company.

He walked fast, turning his collar up against the cold, cradling the bottle in the crook of his arm. It seemed a lot longer than noon since he'd walked off from work. Seemed more like days. And he couldn't believe he'd be going back in the morning either, same as always. What did a person do? Shoot a man in the middle of the night, and then punch in at work the next morning at eight like nothing had happened? Then again, by daylight he could be behind bars, stripped even of his shoelaces.

When he got inside Friendly's, one look told him there wasn't anybody there he knew. Lot of high school kids, looked like, and a few couples with little children, taking them out for an ice cream.

It disappointed him a little, having to eat at a table all by himself, but who did he know in that town anyway? The city where he worked was fifteen miles away, and the only connection he had with the town was that he rented a farmhouse five miles in the country. Did rent. Didn't even do that anymore.

He slid into a booth next to the door and faced the counter so he could watch the waitresses. Right off he spotted the one he'd keep his eye on: a redhead with a way of giving her head a little jerk every now and then to toss her hair back off her shoulders. There was a stuck-up look about her that appealed to him. He was often drawn to women who looked like they'd offer a little challenge.

When he first started taking notice of Lenora,

that was the thing that attracted him to her. That stuck-up way she had. Not unfriendly. Choosey. Hard to get. There were other girls—big-breasted, good-natured ones—who were sweet on him and would have been tickled to death to go to the picture show at the Gem some Saturday night or to the Pea Ridge–Rogers football game with him. But they weren't the ones that caught his eye. Naturally he had to fall for one of the Hokie girls even though he knew all three of them had a reputation for being stuck-up. Cock teasers. That was the word passed around in the boys' locker room.

Even though his mother had made a point of never interfering in his affairs—not after he was grown, anyhow—she could not restrain herself from offering one word of what he later took to be warning. He remembered it clearly, later, although it wouldn't at any point have swayed him in his pursuit of Lenora.

One afternoon when they happened to be standing on the porch together keeping an eye on a storm cloud that was building up in the west, his mother remarked to him that Lenora Hokie was a right pretty little girl. "But did you ever notice, Son, how fussy she is about getting herself up even to appear at the grocery store on a Saturday afternoon? Funny thing to me, but those girls who never have a hair out of place make the worst housekeepers. Seems like if they're good at looking after the one thing they can't be bothered about the other."

But when he set his heart on Lenora and asked her to marry him his mother never said another bad word about her. And she didn't later either, not even when it was evident to everybody that her prediction had proved true. But it didn't make any difference to him. He hadn't married Lenora for her housekeeping ability.

It pleased him that it was the redheaded waitress who came over, stuck the menu in front of his face, and plunked a glass of water on the table.

"Coffee?" she asked him, and when he said sure, he'd take some, she set the cup down so hard the coffee sloshed over into the saucer. He liked the way her rump rode high under her short skirt, the cloth pulling tight over one buttock and then the other as she walked away—so smooth she might have been operating on ball bearings.

He wasn't in any hurry and didn't mind studying the menu, reading down one column of offerings and up the next, even though he knew before he opened it up that he would have a hamburger will all the fixings. Pickles, onions, ketchup, french fries, you name it.

Nevertheless, when the redhead came back to his table and stood, looking bored, pencil poised over the order pad, he couldn't resist holding her there a little while, just fooling around, asking her what was on the menu that was particularly good to eat.

She looked at him like he was crazy, tossing her head in that way he liked. "Kind of depends on what you like to eat, doesn't it? I mean how would I know what you think's good and what isn't? I hardly ever eat here myself and when I do I stick with the grilled cheese. Grilled cheese is grilled cheese."

"Well, I'm a hamburger man myself. Bring me one of the hamburgers to start with, and ask me later if I want some dessert. And french fries. Put some french fries on there too."

She'd gone almost before he'd finished talking. Feisty. He imagined that in high school she played basketball. Didn't seem to him the right type to be a cheerleader. She would be too busy paddling her own canoe to want to be bothered about anybody else's.

It was just the way he knew it would be—a little lonesome sitting there eating his hamburger by himself. When he counted up and thought about it, he realized this would be the fifth night in a row he'd had a hamburger for supper. Hamburgers were just what he thought of first. It wasn't that he was so crazy about them. But whatever he ate at a restaurant was better than warming up soup in his apartment. Either he stopped off at Luciano's for a few beers and a hamburger on the way home from work or he went to the little place on the corner and had whatever the special was that night. It was a lonely life, and after just two weeks he was sick of it. Other men in his circumstances might enjoy themselves with a different woman every night, but he didn't feel like celebrating. His heart wasn't in it. For one thing he felt too bitter about Lenora, and for another, he never had played loose with her, not the way she evidently thought he had.

Back in the early days of their marriage, when he was still riding the rodeo circuit, going off to Poteau or Del Rio or Lubbock, there had been two or three women he'd picked up after the shows. All right. More than two or three if you were going to hold a knife over him until he told the truth. But once he and Lenora came up here you could count on the fingers of one hand the times he'd played loose with her. Nothing that amounted to any-thing. Just playing around. That was one of the things that got to him in this business with Lenora. He could maybe have put up with just the occasional lapse out of her, the one night thing. But no. She had to fall in love like a sixteen-year-old. That was what he just couldn't take. Treating him like that made him jealous and mean. It made him feel he'd thrown away twenty years of his life. Like all those years had been nothing but shit.

By the time the redhead brought his hamburger and fries he had worked himself up into a state so he didn't even feel hungry anymore. His stomach had turned to bile and he knew the hamburger wouldn't agree with him, but he ate it anyway, even the onion, taking big, vicious bites and chewing as though he had a quarrel with it.

When he'd finished with the hamburger he ordered a banana split and ate it too, down to and including the last squirt of fake cream. But sooner or later, no matter how much food he ate, he was going to have to go out there and sit in the cold waiting for the haircutter, freezing his balls off.

He could see the redhead watching him out of the corner of her eye and thought, Oh, hell. If he played his cards right he could make a play for her. He could kid around for a while and ask what she was doing when she finished work. But he just didn't have the patience to go through all that. Not tonight. Not with all this other stuff on his mind.

He scooped up the last bit of syrup from the banana split and went to pay, watching the redhead the whole time. She was cute all right. Maybe on some other night when he wasn't so busy he'd come back and fool around with her. But then it came to him—what he was planning to do that night—and he decided he must be crazy. Behind bars, which was where he stood a good chance of being by morning, he wasn't going to get loose to chase any kind of woman for a long time. So he just gave the redhead a wink in passing and went on out into the cold.

Lenora

IT seemed like she got slower and slower, with so many things to do and feeling so tired from the start. Took her forever just to get through washing and drying the dishes. And the dishes were just the beginning. It was a help, though, having the girls for company while they sat at the kitchen table doing their homework. Or Adele doing hers, writing over a math paper some boy on the school bus had torn up.

It made the work go easier, having somebody to talk to.

"I bet it was just because he's sweet on you," she told Adele. "That boy on the bus."

It was going to be fun in a few years, joking around with Adele about boys, but Adele wasn't old enough yet. She was just a kid—different from the way Lenora had been at eleven. Adele had never given a boy a second look. Not to hear her tell it, at least. But Lenora could well remember the little boyfriend she'd had in first grade. Still remembered his name. Billy Gene Butler. There he stood, his hair damp from where his mother had combed it down before school. Freckles across his nose, and a red spot on his arm where a chigger had gotten him. But Adele wasn't turned like her. Adele put her time in on her lessons, not a bit the way her mother had been in school.

"He better not be sweet on me or I'll kill him," Adele said. "I hate and despise Donny Schultz and I hope he dies."

Sometimes it shocked Lenora, the way Adele talked. Her own mother would have slapped the fire out of her if she'd made remarks like that. But she was more easygoing than her mother had been.

"No you don't, honey," she told Adele. "But you shouldn't say things like that about anybody. Bad thoughts have a way of coming right back at you is what my mother always told me."

"I hope a bus runs over him," Adele said.

Lenora started mopping the floor, giving it a lick and a promise. If she cleaned the middle it would probably be good enough. She couldn't see Charles going into the kitchen just to check on how well she'd mopped it.

She stopped for a minute and brushed the bangs back from Martha's eyes. "Look at your poor little sister," she told Adele. "Sitting right there going to sleep. Hadn't you better finish that on up, Adele, and go to bed? Martha won't go up till you do."

"I got to get this done," Adele said. She was sitting like a little grasshopper, her knees poking out on either side of the chair.

"I wish all I had to do was homework. After I get

this room done, I've still got the living room. And it's in the worst mess."

"I don't know why you're doing all this cleaning tonight for," Adele said, not looking up from her book. "It's been like this for weeks."

Lenora gave her a sharp look, but as far as she could tell Adele didn't mean anything by the remark.

"I can't stand living in a pigsty any longer. Isn't that a good enough reason?"

Adele was chewing on her eraser, her homework in a neat pile. Some question was on the tip of her tongue; Lenora could see her deciding whether or not to ask it.

"If you were going to go somewhere a long way off and you didn't have the money to get there, how would you do it?" Adele finally asked. "If you *had* to go?"

It wasn't a question Lenora was expecting, and it took her a few seconds to come up with the answer. "Why, I don't know. If I *had* to get somewhere—if it was a matter of life or death and I didn't have any money—I'd have to hitchhike I guess. But that isn't anything for you to do, honey. Not ever. I'd be worried sick if you tried a thing like that. It would just be if I had to get somewhere and there wasn't any other way."

Adele was a funny one, the questions she came up with. There were times when she seemed to know as much as a grown-up, as much as somebody thirty years old, and then she would ask some simple thing that made you see she wasn't anything but a child after all.

"If you're done with your homework you go on

up to bed now," she told Adele. Martha was sound asleep in her chair.

"If I do, will you come up too? Come tell us good night in bed?"

"Oh, honey, I've got so much to do."

But when she looked at Adele's face she knew she'd have to do it, she'd have to go up and kiss them good night at least.

"You go on up and take Martha with you. See she brushes her teeth. And when you're in bed I'll come up for a minute."

Adele was as good with Martha as she was, the way Adele took Martha by the hand and led her up the stairs with Martha walking in her sleep.

While the girls were climbing the stairs she got the vacuum cleaner out and started on the rug. But it wasn't picking up the way it was supposed to. Broken, probably, like everything else around there. But she thought that maybe if she just managed to stir the dust around a little the rug would look better than it did.

What she wouldn't do for Charles. It was laughable when she thought about it. She might never have gotten around to cleaning the house if it hadn't been for him. Adele was right. And there she was, nervous as a girl, trying to make everything pretty for her sweetheart.

In spite of how tired she was and knowing too she might not get a wink of sleep all night long, she started humming, smiling to herself. It made all the difference in the world doing something because you wanted to do it. After she got finished with the living room she'd take a bath and make herself pretty. She'd try to lie down and get some rest before Charles got there. She wondered if she'd

have time to do her hair—to wash and put it up—
but decided she wouldn't. One thing she didn't
want was for Charles to arrive while she still had
her hair in curlers. And she didn't have any guar-
antee about what time he'd get there. So that was
out. Her hair would just have to rest on the washing and setting she'd given it the day before.

As she headed for the stairs she noticed there was
no light burning above the garage, so the boys
were out, as usual. She worried about them, about
the life they led, but if Burl was going to wash his
hands of the whole affair what could she do? The
boys were past the time now when they'd pay any
attention to what their mother said to them. They
needed the firm hand of a father. Scott was
grown-up at eighteen, and Jeff tagged right behind
Scott, following everything he did just like a
shadow. He always had. Just two years between
them and they'd always been close as thieves. But
it upset her when Jeff dropped out of high school
just because Scott was out of school. Or at least she
thought that was the reason. Jeff never would say.
It was a mystery to her.

When he was in grade school Jeff got good re-
port cards. He was just like Adele in that. But later
on he quit trying. Or that was the way it looked.
Jeff's teachers had called them in—her and Burl—
last year when Jeff was in tenth grade. Nice people,
she thought, who seemed to have Jeff's best inter-
ests at heart. They said he had the potential to do
real well; he could do what he wanted if he'd just
give it a try. But the trouble was he'd just quit
trying. If Jeff didn't change his downward course
he would fail in every subject, even including
physical education. She hadn't understood how it

would be possible to fail physical education if you had two good legs. But Jeff had managed to do it. Clean sweep. Every single subject. So this year, when he turned sixteen he just wouldn't go back. Said he was finished and that was that. So there hadn't been a thing she or Burl could do with him, and at least he got a job in the garage where Scott worked. Jeff had always been good with his hands. And if could support himself at sixteen, why shouldn't he go ahead and do it? But she couldn't make up her mind about this, about whether or not Jeff should've dropped out. School had never done *her* much good, so she could see how Jeff might've gotten his fill. But she wanted him to get ahead in life—better than she had—and dropping out of high school sure didn't seem like a very good start.

Still, the whole thing was out of her hands. Once the boys were buying their own food, there went any little hold she and Burl might have over them. They were the same as grown men even if they were young. Sometimes it was hard for her to remember when the boys were little, or that they ever had been. That part of her life was finished and done with. Only Martha was still a little girl, and she didn't have much time to give even to Martha. The best she could do was barely keep their heads afloat. She did well to get something to eat on the table and clean clothes on their backs. At least she was doing that much.

On the way up the stairs she picked up toys the girls had strewn about. They might have been there for days, those very same Barbie dolls, but Lenora hadn't noticed them before. Now she saw everything with Charles's eyes, and she wanted everything to be just right.

The girls had left the door of their bedroom open and she peeked in. There they were with both their heads on the same pillow the way they always slept. When they were smaller she used to scoot them over once they were asleep. It didn't seem to her they would rest well lying so their arms and legs might get mixed up together in the night, but now she let them be. When she thought about it, she could remember that she and Pearl used to do the very same thing. She had once waked up holding on to Pearl's hair with both hands, though Pearl, sound asleep, hadn't noticed a thing.

She brought up the covers under the girls' chins and patted the lumps their feet made. Martha's eyes were already half asleep, blue eyes like hers with long lashes.

"Good night, sweetheart."

Martha made a kissing noise, kissing the air. Missing her cheek.

Adele was watching with those brown eyes of hers, a throwback to some distant relative. Skinny the way Lenora had been when she was a girl, but that thin little face and those brown eyes didn't come from her. That dark complexion either.

Adele just lay still when she was kissed, not making a move to kiss back though she was the one who'd insisted on being told good night. But you couldn't tell with Adele. Never could, not even when she was a tiny little thing. Adele always did have a head of her own. Turned funny, as they'd say down home. But she was a good girl. A regular little mother. Just solemn, that was all.

Adele watched, never taking her eyes off Lenora's face, studying her like there was something on the tip of her tongue.

"You want anything, honey?"

But Adele wouldn't answer. She just kept her eyes on Lenora's face till it made her nervous.

"Well, good night," she told Adele from the door as she clicked off the light. "Sleep tight. Don't let the bedbugs bite."

Adele never said a word. But Lenora could still feel her looking. Even with the door shut she could feel Adele's eyes resting on the back of her head. She would never know what was taking place inside that child's mind.

Still, as soon as she shut the door of the girls' room she put them out of her head and felt happiness go through her like a warm drink on a cold day. The worst of the chores were over, and now what she had to do was take a bath and make herself pretty. She still had time to get everything just right before Charles came.

Grace

Every night, sitting on the couch in front of the tv, Virgil fell asleep. Snored too. It didn't matter what was on, nothing could hold him more than fifteen minutes. "Hee Haw," Dick Van Dyke, whatever. He wasn't much company sprawled out there with his head resting on the back of the couch, his mouth wide open. She used to be afraid he might swallow his teeth some night with his mouth open like that, but now she'd gotten used to the way he sat and didn't figure he was going to pass to his Maker that way, by choking on his teeth. Sometimes she gave his leg a good pinch and said "Virgil!" in his ear to get his attention, but even if he opened his eyes and sat up—"Must've just dropped off for a minute"—he'd be snoring again before she could even ask him a question.

Virgil's life had been hard and he was tired, no doubt about that, but her life hadn't been any flowery bed of ease either, and she was still struggling along. Men just didn't have the endurance women did. They played out sooner. There were a lot more widow women around than there were widowers. In her own case, though, she wouldn't take any bets she'd outlive Virgil. The doctor had told her she had high blood pressure, and she well knew herself that heart trouble ran in her family. The last time she was at the doctor's she'd told him about those palpitations she had when her heart took off, felt like, trying to do something funny like skip rope. The doctor got out that little bell-shaped thing and listened but didn't appear to think much of what he heard. Just patted her on the back and told her she ought to be good for another twenty years. Not that she believed it. Doctors were always joking around trying to make you feel good.

Some man wearing a broad-brimmed hat came on "Hee Haw" and told a joke about a chicken. Something to do with a rooster and an egg, but she couldn't quite catch it. Everybody in the audience laughed, though, so it must have been a funny joke.

She poked Virgil with her elbow and bent over to shout in his ear. "You catch what that was, Virgil? The joke that man told?"

But Virgil just sucked in on his teeth and made a noise in his throat that could have meant anything.

Sometimes she got real lonesome, sitting around there at night with Virgil sound asleep. She got to worrying about things and thinking back on the past, which wasn't a good habit to fall into. And tonight there was something weighing on her spirit. She didn't know what it was, but she thought it had to do with one of her kin. It was something bad about somebody, only she didn't know just what. Wouldn't come clear to her. But all day she'd had a sinking feeling, and it had affected her health too. Several times in the day her heart had done that racing or skipping or whatever it was it did, and she'd had to sit on the sofa until she could catch her breath. Something weighed her down, seemed like. Some burden to carry.

She pushed herself up off the couch now and went over and turned down the sound on "Hee Haw" so she couldn't hear it anymore. Because of her blood pressure her hearing had gone bad and it didn't seem worthwhile to try to catch the jokes. But the pictures could keep her company. She liked to be reminded that there were other people in the world besides her and Virgil, and him asleep.

At least with the noise turned off she might be able to hear herself think so she could try to figure out what it was bothering her.

She sat heavily on the couch, just letting go when she'd positioned herself in the middle. Her joints had gone bad on her, and anyway she'd gotten so fat. Couldn't bend and move around the way she used to could.

Virgil rose in the air as she hit the couch and then he settled back just the way he had been. Didn't rouse.

Now that she was sitting again, she tried to think. Who was it, what trouble was there weighing on her spirit tonight? In her mind she made the rounds. First there was Frank and his family three miles down the road. A cow had stepped on Frank's foot earlier in the week and turned it black-and-blue. For a few days Frank had hobbled around something pitiful, but he was better now.

Nothing wrong with Frank or his family that seemed to warrant special worry. And Lester was fine. She and Virgil had been over there the day before yesterday and found Marylou making sausage. Gave them some for their breakfast and it was right good, only a little heavy on the pepper for her taste.

Going on down through the children and grand-children she hesitated a few minutes over Jolene's youngest boy, Byron. Byron was just old enough to take the car out, and of course he was driving them crazy wanting to use it. Last time he got it he'd taken a whole carload of young people out to Blue Mountain Lake and they hadn't gotten back until two in the morning. When they arrived home none of them had shoes on. They'd every one left their shoes sitting in a line at the water's edge. Now Jolene and Herman wouldn't let Byron have the car again for a long time, and he was giving them grief over it. But she didn't believe it was Byron and the car that was weighing her down tonight. It was something she hadn't come to yet.

Then she got to the bottom of the list, reaching Burl and his family in her considerations, and knew by the heartsick feeling that came over her it was Burl all right and had been Burl all along. Maybe that was why she'd put him off to last. Not a word out of him or Lenora for over a month now. They hadn't ever been good letter writers, but they generally did better than that. Burl hardly ever sat down and wrote—it was Lenora if it was anybody— but there hadn't been anything out of either one of them.

Bad news travels fast. So it couldn't be anybody

dead or they would have been sure to hear that.
Whatever it was it couldn't be the worst. But there
could be somebody down bad sick. Or it could be
any number of other things—all the troubles that
might not seem worthwhile putting in a letter.

Oh, but it had always been Burl. Burl who'd
given her more heartache than all the others put
together. The youngest one often did turn out that
way. You spoiled them because you loved them too
much. By the time you had the last one you knew
how quick they grew up, what a short time you had
them little and sweet. And by that time you were
worn out too and slower on your feet. You didn't
get after the youngest the way you did the oldest.
The youngest naturally got by with more. And
Burl had been such a pretty little boy, the only one
of hers that was curly-headed. And those big eyes.
She could still remember, just as plain, Burl sitting
astride the old log fence pretending like he was
riding it, waving that little lariat Virgil made for
him, rocking back and forth there by the hour. He
always was taken with horses, just like Virgil when
he was a young man. They'd been close, those two.
Once upon a time they had. Apple of his daddy's
eye. Well, hers too. She had to admit it. With that
last one you just let go, just didn't do the way you
should. One child you just wanted to enjoy. One
child you wanted the sweetness from. Oh, she'd
broken many a switch over Burl's little legs—it
wasn't that she hadn't—but her heart had never
been in it. She'd let him off light, never could re-
fuse Burl anything if he cried for it, and he knew
that well. Children always knew how to get what
they wanted out of their momma and daddy. And

yet for all the love they'd poured out on Burl, he had to grow up to cause them grief in their old age.

What she hated the worst, what gave her the most cause for grief, was the way he wouldn't go to church after he was about twelve or thirteen. Just as soon as he felt himself becoming a man he'd said no. Wouldn't go back and there hadn't been anything she could do. No amount of praying or scolding had done any good. The Hokies, Lenora's folks, hadn't ever been ones for going to church much so it wasn't surprising that Lenora hadn't been firm in her faith. She couldn't blame Lenora as much as she did Burl that their children all grew up without the Word, like heathens in some far country. Burl just hadn't done right by his family. She would have to say it although it hurt her soul. But it was a shame the way Burl had failed to take those children of his to Sunday school. Poor little things didn't stand a chance. She'd done what she could, taken them to church every chance she got, given them ever one Bibles of their own. She'd tried to sow the word of God in their hearts though she doubted if it had taken root, falling as it did on a stony ground.

But seemed like, when they were little things and she'd taken them off with her to the Mt. Judah Baptist, they had listened better than most children did. She could remember Jeff especially, keeping his eyes on one particular window—the one showing Lazarus coming forth from the tomb. He had been real taken with that picture. Could look at it for hours on end. There he would sit, just as still as could be, his eyes never budging from Lazarus's face.

There was something about Jeff that always touched her heart. Maybe it was because he tended to get overlooked with a big brother and later on a little sister and then another to look after. Jeff was the one you might forget about since he was such a quiet child. Never two words to say for himself. But those eyes of his. He didn't miss a thing, Jeff didn't. She could still remember whispering in his ear, "You're my boy, aren't you, Jeff?" and how he would put his arms around her neck and give it a squeeze.

It wouldn't surprise her any if Jeff grew up to become a preacher. Oh, she knew he probably wasn't thinking along those lines now, but he was only half grown. There was lots of time yet. She could remember so well coming across him out behind the big walnut tree, saying a funeral service over Adele when she wasn't much more than a baby. There she lay in the grass, her eyes closed and her hands clasped over her stomach. When she first saw Adele lying like that it gave her a turn, though she knew it was just a game. The kinds of things children get up to. Jeff was standing beside her as solemn as could be, holding a book out in front of him like it was a Bible—had it upside down as she recalled—and saying—it just came into her head, she just recollected what he'd said, it was so funny: "Now I lay me down to sleep, I pray the Lord my soul to keep." That was the only prayer the poor child knew. But he did know you were supposed to say words over someone who'd passed on, though where he had picked up that knowledge she would give a penny to know.

It came to her that it was Jeff weighing so heavily on her soul that night, with troubles that she couldn't know. Yet through all that distance it was his need speaking out to her, his granny, a poor old woman helpless to do any more than pray.

She groaned with the pain of it. How much old people felt for those they loved, and how little they could do!

Her Bible lay on the end table where she could get to it easily. Every night she read a little before she went to bed. So she lifted it from the table and picked up the glasses she needed to make out the words.

That Bible had been with her from the time she was a girl. A present from her sweet mother on her sixteenth birthday, on the day she became a woman grown. The black leather was worn to brown now through all the times she'd held it in her hands. How many times the good book had helped her when her heart was troubled! It had gotten her through her life this far, and she knew it would see her home.

She slipped her glasses behind her ears and held the book in her hands, letting its spine rest in the palm of one hand, allowing the pages to open out to whatever passage they would. That was the way she let God's will be known to her. She held the book in her hands, but God chose the place for it to open. The words her eyes fell on were always the words she needed to hear the most. Time after time she had proven this to be true.

Now the book opened in her hand and she bent forward, settling her glasses so she could read.

It was John 12:29 her eye lit on, and this line: *An angel spake to him.*

She looked down again and saw the line standing out clearly. But what was she supposed to make of those words? They certainly did not seem to be clear. "What does that mean, Lord?" she asked, but although she waited, trying to clear her mind, listening for the message to come through, she remained baffled. Maybe it meant she was right and Jeff was chosen as a minister of God. It could mean that. Jeff was on the point of hearing his calling and would know it soon. It would be like an angel spoke into his ear telling him what he was supposed to do.

But she was not completely satisfied by this answer. So she let her eyes wander up the page until they came to verse 24—one she knew by heart—and as soon as she saw it she said the words without bothering to look down: *Verily, verily, I say unto you, except a corn of wheat fall into the ground and die, it abideth alone: but if it die, it bringeth forth much fruit.*

Maybe this was the verse she had been meant to see all along. If it was verse 24 that was the right one, then she thought it might be a hopeful message that concerned Burl more than Jeff. It was Burl's old pride and stubbornness that was the corn of wheat. She felt sure of this now. That was just the way Burl was, abiding alone, not letting God or anybody else help him. But if he would bow that pride, if he would let it fall from him and die like a corn of wheat falling to the ground, how much fruit could be brought forth. Burl's life and the lives of all his family could be saved at last, and she wouldn't have to grieve herself in the middle of the night the way she had to now. She could go to her grave in peace if all was well with her children and their children after them.

"I thank you, Lord," she said out loud, through

Virgil's snoring. All the time she was watching the faces of the people on "Hee Haw," gathered to sing some song together, their mouths opening and shutting all at the same time though not a sound came out.

Jeff

I<small>F</small> it hadn't been that they went out to get that pizza—he and Scott—they would never have met Karen and Amy. The short one, Karen, had a round face and curly hair, not bad looking. But the one called Amy was wearing a jacket that had Johns River Eagles written on white against a bright-blue background, and she would have been his pick because of the word *Eagles* emblazoned across her back. There was something mysterious about that word. He thought of razor-sharp talons and beaks like steel.

There was nothing interesting about Karen, the one with the round, simple face. He knew she was the kind always asking questions: "Where do you go to school? What year are you? Oh, you work? Well, where do you work, then? Listen, which do you like better—The Who or the Doors? Which record of theirs? Do you know Mike Halloran who plays basketball for Blakely? Well, maybe you know Johnnie White? Real tall guy rides a Honda around town?"

She could probably keep it up for hours without a break, nursing her vanilla soda along, taking a tiny little sip every once in a while. She and that friend of hers had probably been sitting in that same booth, drinking sodas and putting on weight around their hips for two hours, just waiting for a couple of guys to come in and take notice of them. He had sized them up right away. Two losers, both kind of funny looking. But it wasn't their looks so much that made him give Scott a warning look. It was because they laughed too much and kept cutting their eyes too often to the booth where he and Scott were sitting. It disgusted him when things like that happened. And tonight he wanted to think his own thoughts without having to struggle to remember to be ordinary Jeff who sized up girls and talked about what kind of pizza to order.

Then when Scott did this stupid thing of stacking all the objects on the table on top of one another, the ashtray and the container that held sugar and the salt-and-pepper shaker, ending with as many packages of sugar as he could coax into balance—reaching as high as five before the whole thing toppled as of course it was bound to do—those two girls laughed as though it was the funniest thing they ever saw. Everybody in the Pizza Kitchen turned around to stare, to see what the joke was. He couldn't stand girls who laughed like that, and he couldn't stand the way Scott was showing off, catching their eye.

"Those're two dummies," he said to Scott, leaning far over the table to catch his attention. "We don't need those two. If you want to pick up some-body we can do better than that."

But Scott kept his head turned the whole time, winking or making some kind of face at the girls across Jeff's shoulder even while Jeff was telling him to stop it. So when Scott slid out of the booth and sauntered over to the girls' table, making his move, Jeff just sat where he was, saying, "Oh, shit," under his breath.

He *knew* Scott would maneuver the one with the Eagles jacket into his side of the booth and of course he did, leaving the other one to crowd beside him, giggling.

He kicked Scott under the table, a good heavy blow to his shin, but Scott didn't even blink in his direction. He was too busy sliding the pizza around so the girls could reach it, and they did, slipping their fingers underneath the crust and squealing when some of the hot cheese topping brushed against their hands. Both girls aimed their remarks in the direction of the pizza or at each other, gig-gling at some joke they held between them.

If Karen hadn't been blocking his way out of the booth, Jeff would have gotten up immediately. He knew exactly how the rest of it would go. And it bored him so much he felt he might have to put his head down on top of the pizza plate and go to sleep.

First they would have to sit there eating the pizza and drinking sodas for another twenty or thirty minutes. After that, they might get as far as the video games where they would fool around for a while longer, he and Scott playing Space Invaders and the girls watching, squealing and clapping them on; or else the girls would play a machine themselves, making a mess of it. Another thirty minutes could go that way. A certain amount of time had to pass before Scott could make the next move, before he could ask very casually if the girls would like to go for a ride. Would they like to buy some beer and take it out to the lake? And then if there were no hitches, if everything went along just the way it was supposed to—why then, after a few beers or whatever, Scott would take off driving again, fast, telling the girls there was another place they ought to see before they went home. A place they owed it to themselves to see.

Of course the girls would be tipsy by then from the beer which they would not be used to drinking in spite of the casual way they'd act about the whole thing, and he and Scott would have gotten them softened up for the next thing. Already they would have kissed them a few times, felt them up a little—nothing too serious, just a little rubbing up that the girls would have started getting really into by now. And with the beer their better judgment, if they had any to start with, would already have left them. The final and last step would not be difficult. The last step would be disgustingly easy, in fact. Jeff could never get over how easy it was, no matter how many times he and Scott had played this game. It was so predictable—how the girls always went along. How they would go up the steps to the room over the garage without any objection at all. Usually, right at the last, with the door closed and locked and he and Scott getting busy on the zippers and hooks and buttons and whatever, they would put up a little bit of objection. *This* hadn't been what they'd intended at all. They'd been tricked. But Scott had explained all of this to

Jeff, and he understood it now as the truth—all this was done to establish the girls' alibi so to speak. If their mothers and fathers were watching this scene they would see that their daughters had objected, had put up a fight, but had been overcome by superior force.

A few kisses, a little bit of laying on of hands in the right places, and that flurry of objection was easily overcome.

After that, the girls could say they'd been raped if it made them feel any better about it. What mattered was that from that point there was no challenge. The next problem was getting the girls ready to leave when the time came. They hardly ever wanted to leave. By then they had worked out alibis for their parents ("We went out driving with Patti's sister and the car broke down. We had to *walk* ten miles, for heaven's sake. What do you mean a telephone? There wasn't even a filling station, much less a telephone"). What he and Scott had to do was practically dress the girls and haul them to their feet.

But tonight there were other things on his mind. There was something about Adele, about what Adele had said, that he wanted to turn over in his mind. Why should Adele have been the one to see the shadow of the angel of death, and not him? For a long time he'd felt he was close to seeing through the mystery. With birds, with cats, it hadn't been any good. There had been nothing more than that sudden dulling of their eyes. Perhaps for animals there was only the quick, enveloping darkness. He had to see more.

"I got to go to the bathroom," he said suddenly. Scott looked at him in surprise, and the girls turned their heads away as though they'd never heard of such a thing as a bathroom in their lives.

"Well, if you gotta go you gotta go is what I always say," Scott said, making one of his silly faces, trying to pass the whole thing off as a joke. The girls dutifully laughed although a little of the edge of excitement had slipped from their voices. They both stared at Jeff as Karen slid far enough from the bench to let him pass.

Once he got away from the table he never looked back. He walked in front of the counter, passed out of sight behind some giant plastic bamboo tree, and went through the side door. It would be a five-mile walk home, but he didn't care.

Until he passed through the town he walked, but as soon as he reached the highway and began moving into the country he started to run. He hadn't run in a long time, not since he was in junior high and on the track team. He had forgotten how it was, how his lungs slowly eased so he could breathe more deeply, how his muscles began moving in that way that reminded him of a well-oiled engine. He had liked being on the track team and had never complained about the long runs they were obliged to make in the afternoons when school was out, keeping all together, running around and around the playing fields, beating down the same tufts of dandelion and grass as they passed.

If he had liked it so much, why had he quit? When he thought about it, he knew he'd quit the team and quit school for the same reason he'd left the Pizza Kitchen that night. There was some knowledge he had that he must act on, some urging he couldn't go against. He had to be left alone to let his mind float—like a hawk circling a field—

over those questions that enthralled him. For a long
time he'd known he wasn't like other people. He
was concerned with things that others never
thought about. Even before he had removed himself physically from school or from the Pizza
Kitchen that night, he had taken the part of himself that was important and had put it in some
distant place.

Now as he ran along the side of the highway, the
passing cars giving him enough light to see by, he
let his mind settle into the rhythm of his running.
There was the Jeff the others thought they knew,
the one who worked in the garage and joked
around with Scott. The one who picked up girls
and drove around in the country drinking beer.
That Jeff was in the upper part of his head, in
some space that was simple and bright. It wasn't
any trouble to live in that space if he wanted to.
He could joke with the guys at the garage. He
could make out with girls. He could do all the
things he was supposed to do, as though he'd put
himself on automatic pilot and was sleepwalking
through the day.

But there were also the secret and precious
things he didn't share with anybody. It made him
feel powerful, having these two ways of being.

He was impressed by the story he read in the
newspaper about some kid who carried a rifle to
the roof of a building and then picked people off
down below in the street. People the kid didn't
even know, just people who happened to be in the
wrong place at the wrong time. And the story he
read once about a boy who killed a little neighbor
girl and put the body in this strange place: in the
back room of a church, stuffed inside a trunk used

to store old hymnbooks. The thing that held Jeff's attention was that when these deeds came to light and the murderers were caught, everybody who knew them was terribly shocked. Everybody went on record saying what a good, well-mannered boy the killer was. How he'd always been so quiet and well behaved, always saying hello to old people and doing favors for neighborhood children. Getting their kites into the air or teaching them how to bat a ball.

He thought about these stories, turning them over and over in his mind. There were questions he would like somebody to answer. For instance, had the people who committed the murders known all along that they had two different ways of being and one of them secret? Had they known during the time they were saying good morning to old women and running with kites that one day they were going to kill somebody? How would it be to look into your eyes in a mirror and know they were the eyes of a murderer, or of someone who planned murder and would one day, when the time was right, carry it out? And all the time, while you were preparing the way, everyone was busy saying what a good boy you were. What a nice boy.

Or, maybe, did the murderer start taking shape behind the person's eyes without him knowing? Could he look into his own eyes and see nothing unusual, so that the other self, when it emerged, came as a surprise to him too?

It made Jeff laugh as he ran, thinking about the look that would have come over Karen's face if he had asked her these questions while she licked pizza sauce from her fingers.

It was no wonder he had to keep quiet about the

things that intrigued him. Scott would never know why he'd left. Scott would really be pissed off for a little while, but he'd manage all right. Somehow he would accommodate two girls or he'd find someone else for Karen. Scott might think he'd left because he didn't want to get stuck with Karen. That was the kind of thing Scott would think. But Karen had nothing to do with it, of course. It was just that he wanted to close down that boring upper part of his mind and drift down into the other.

From a distance he could see the farmhouse with the upstairs lights burning. There was one on in his mother's bedroom and one on downstairs so that the house appeared to be busily occupied. But this was only an illusion. There was nothing to see as he passed, turning his head to look in the windows as some stranger might. His mother had pulled down the shades in her room, and the girls were probably asleep. Downstairs, although he could see into the living room, the light burned on emptiness. He was the outsider looking in, the stranger passing in the night wondering if *this* was the house, if this was the one awaiting his entry.

Lenora

She'd remembered to leave a light burning in the living room, thank goodness, so she wouldn't have to go down there again. Now that she was upstairs she could stay there. The house was clean as she was going to get it, and with just one dim light burning, Charles probably couldn't tell much about the living room as he passed through. Surely he would have better things on his mind than her housekeeping as he made his way to the stairs.

What she liked was a bathtub so full of water it reached right up to her breasts. And she was lavish with the lavender bath-oil beads, sprinkling them all across the surface of the water so they would make her smell good and would keep her skin from getting dry. After growing up the way she had, she would always think of a bathtub full of water as a luxury. When she was a child she had one bath a week in a zinc bathtub behind the stove. Hot water came from the tea kettle and cold water from a bucket. There was barely enough water to cover her toes when she was sitting, shivering, in the tub.

Before she climbed into the bath she put cream on her face so her skin would be as smooth as a baby's. There was so much work to do just keeping yourself up, and she didn't have time to devote to it as she should. There were women who came to get their hair fixed at the shop who probably spent two hours every day just keeping themselves looking good. It was amazing how many things you ought to do if you did everything you could. Consider feet, for instance. She was on hers too much and the skin on the soles had gotten thick from all the walking she did. She ought to take pumice to those calluses, but she wouldn't do that tonight. There were other parts of her body that worried her more. Her elbows. Whenever she got a glimpse of her elbows it gave her a shock to see how wrinkled they were—like the hide of an old elephant. It was hard to do right by her hands too, since she had to have them in water so much of the time.

You could always tell by a woman's hands how hard she had to work. There were women she knew who had hands so white and soft it looked like they'd never been used. So pampered and taken care of. White and smooth as milk. But she would never have hands like that.

The good points she had were those she came by naturally. Her face was firm and the line under her chin was still tight. That was always a sure sign— that loosening under the chin. And those fine lines that started working their way into the skin around your neck. They slipped up on you more easily than crow's feet did. Everybody knew about crow's feet and how you had to use a good cream around your eyes at night, but a lot of women didn't seem to know they had those other little lines.

Not much got past her, though, working at the job she did. She had her hands on other women's hair and skin all day long, and there was nothing that could escape her scrutiny when she had some woman lying back with her head in the sink. Everything was clearly visible to someone standing a foot away. Every clogged pore, every line. She could pinpoint a woman's age down to the year. No matter what good care a woman took of herself there were telltale signs that couldn't be hidden.

For thirty-eight she looked good. And that was an expert's opinion. Hardly anybody would judge her to be more than thirty-four. She'd swear it. Yet she could see the signs and clues if she looked real close.

The human body has a natural attraction for the earth, the way it starts sagging toward it so early on. This was something that depressed her. By the time you came to die you had already given in, had already practically slid into the grave. And yet people didn't feel as old as they looked. Your head never seemed to know what the rest of your body was up too, as though the one wasn't on speaking terms with the other.

There was a brown hair, curling around one of her nipples, that she was going to have to remember to pull out with tweezers. And while she was at it she'd better check on her eyebrows too when she got out of the bath. It was shocking how fast eyebrows could grow. She'd heard somewhere that even after you died things like your hair and your fingernails kept right on growing. They were the last to get the message, down there in the dark. It gave her a creepy feeling to think about it.

It was her hair that Charles had noticed first. He always noticed hair—women's hair at least— and hers was remarkable because it was natural blond and had remained so light in color. She had never put a thing on it. She hadn't had to. Anyone looking at it casually, anyone who wasn't in the business, might well think she put a little bleach on it from time to time. But she didn't. Charles had seen that right away. They had been standing in the bank, waiting to get to one of the tellers. She'd been in front of him and had known he was look- ing, giving her more than a casual going-over, though she'd pretended she didn't notice a thing. She'd pretended she was standing there with her head in the clouds and a little smile on her lips as though she had good and exciting things to look forward to. But she'd known he was behind her, looking.

Of course she knew who he was. It was impos- sible not to know Mr. Charles, at least by sight, if you were a hairdresser in this town. Mr. Charles Salon was well known, and she had seen him more than once coming out of the door of his shop, al- ways in a hurry, as though there were a great many important things he had to keep up with.

She tried to be at her ease as she felt his eyes on her, and she turned her face just the slightest bit in his direction to give him the benefit of her best side.

Then when she turned around and smiled she made sure to look straight into his eyes so he wouldn't be able to slide out of it. Not that he seemed to want to. He smiled right back and said to please excuse him. He supposed it was rude to stare as he'd been staring, but she did have a most beautiful head of hair. And that was a professional's opinion.

As though it was the most natural thing in the world, he reached out a hand and touched her hair, running his fingers through it slowly. He might have been touching something precious from the way he acted. A shiver went down her spine where she stood, right there in the bank. That was the way a cat felt, being stroked. She didn't want it to stop and could have shut her eyes and moved her head against his hand, not caring a bit what anybody in the bank might think.

"You shouldn't be tempted to use highlights on that hair of yours," he told her. "Highlights won't do the texture any good. What you ought to use is a mild shampoo and a light conditioner. Nothing else. And I can tell you your hair will stay fair and thick until you're an old, old woman. You don't know how lucky you are."

But she did know. At that moment, smiling into Charles's face, she knew she was the luckiest woman on earth.

When Charles said, "How about going over to the Marriott for a quick cup of coffee?" she didn't hesitate. It seemed the most natural thing.

Only later she realized it might have sounded as though she was in the habit of going off for coffee with men she'd just met. But the truth was entirely different. Whatever others might do—and she heard plenty of the details of other women's love lives in the shop—she had always considered that for her married was married. It hadn't seriously entered her head to be tempted by some man other than Burl although, goodness knows, she'd had opportunities if she'd wanted to take them. It just seemed there was some little voice in her head telling her that carrying on with another man wasn't for her. But when Charles asked her to go with him for that cup of coffee, the little voice didn't have a word to say.

She had to admit that it was Charles's good looks that got to her from the first. That thick, wavy hair and those deep-brown eyes. Nose straight as a ruler. Elegant. Everything about him was elegant. Those shirts he wore with the tiny stripes, so small you had to be up close to see them, and those sleek black shoes. He wore his clothes and carried his shoulders like a prince. No wonder he had so much business in his shop. Women couldn't resist him.

Yet in spite of Charles's good looks and his beautiful clothes it was something else too that drew her, though it was not a thing easy to explain. There was something, well, almost shy about him. He was a lot quieter than Burl, for instance. Burl never had been able to shut up in his life. He would talk on and on to anybody, even when they didn't want to hear him. About the last thing you'd say about Burl was that he was shy.

Yet it wasn't that Charles was backward. Nothing like that. He had beautiful manners and could always think of things to say. It was just that when he was with her he seemed more relaxed than he did with other people. His good manners were a way he had of keeping other people at a distance. But with her he laughed and joked around. Like the way he called her Nore, his little whore. Not that he really meant that about being a whore. It was just a joke. But she didn't think he would say that to anyone else.

From the time they had coffee together that morning, she was a goner. She knew that right away and never fought it. It was bound to be. That was the way she thought about it. Why else would they both have been in the bank at the same time that morning? Or why would he have been standing in line right behind her? It was just meant to be, that was all.

But the same way she knew this she also knew that he didn't feel exactly the same about her as she did about him. She thought about him all the time. She couldn't deny it. She thought about him night and day. But he couldn't have thought about her night and day. If he had he would never have made her suffer the way he did. Not that he meant to hurt her. He just had no idea that he could ruin her day by sounding preoccupied or a little distant when she talked to him on the phone. He didn't know about the agonies she went through when he didn't telephone just when he said he would, or when he told her he couldn't come over after all when she'd been banking on seeing him. He didn't know that she was either so miserable she wanted to die or so happy she wished she could. No halfway ground for her. But for him it couldn't be like that. If it was, he'd take pains to relieve her suffering.

Loving Charles was a terrible fix to be in. She knew it. But whatever else anybody offered her—if somebody came up to her and said she could have a fortune in money, either that or Charles, but not both—there wasn't any doubt which she'd choose. Over and over again she'd pick the very state she was in, even though it cost her so much pain.

She would choose him, would choose all of it, if

she couldn't have him any other way. And yet she always came back to this: When Charles left her, as she knew he would, what would happen to her then? Every time this thought came into her head, she felt like she'd just taken a step off the top of a cliff. It was so scary she couldn't bear to think about it.

As she climbed out of the tub and patted herself dry, she did it again. She put all the doubts to one side and thought about only one thing: How much longer would she have to wait before Charles got to the house?

She had two nightgowns that she could wear. One was green and shiny, cut to fit but with a long slit up one side so she could walk in it. The other was white, cut very low in the front and with inserts of lace around the waist. She wished she had a new gown to surprise Charles with, but she couldn't have a new one every time.

Feeling the way she had when she was little and playing at dress-up in her mother's clothes, she tried on each of the gowns, turning from side to side in front of the mirror, fluffing her hair and smiling at herself. The white one made her look sweet and girlish; the green one was more sophisticated. The trouble was in deciding between them. Even when she walked around the room, feeling the cloth so silky against her legs, she couldn't make up her mind. What finally decided her was remembering she'd worn the green one last time. So this time she'd stick with the white. It was fine. In the pink light, propped up on the pillows so she could see herself in the mirror, she looked about twenty. It was a treat, how young and pretty she did look.

Jeff

He seemed to float in darkness although if he tried he could make out the stove, could see a chair and, across the room, his chest of drawers. Outside the windows there was another darkness where tree limbs swayed. Lying on the bed which was pushed next to the glass of the window, he appeared to be suspended between the two darknesses. In the driveway, under the trees, shadows moved.

The outside darkness was heavy, gathering. He could feel it in the air—the beating of wings like the throb of some powerful motor.

Fully clothed, he composed himself on the bed, his hands lying on his stomach. Then, slowly, he shut his eyes and saw yet another darkness—the one inside his head. The one illumined sometimes with dreams. He watched it now, waiting, sorting through the photographs from his collection, examining each face as it passed through his mind, deciding on the one he would think about. One of the joyous ones. One of the faces that brought evidence of the ecstasy, of that vision that cracked the heart.

It was Linnie's face he could not pass by. Hers, always his favorite, he held in his mind and let fill the space behind his eyelids. Her lips parted—it seemed she *must* tell—the words were surely rising in her throat. Yet she had not managed to say but two words, furnishing the only clue he had. *Too bright.* This is what the family said were her last words. *She grew easy at the last* was how the story went, was how it was passed down. *Through the last day she struggled, a hard labor. But toward late afternoon she grew easy. Resting well, it seemed like. And then, when it was getting on to suppertime, she opened her eyes. A look of joy came on her face. What is it, honey?* the family wanted to know. *Do you feel better?* And it was then she had said all she was able to tell them. *Too bright.*

He let her face come clear in his mind and watched the lips part. He wanted so much to pass through with her, to see what she had seen.

But even though he waited, it wouldn't appear. He knew how near it was, how this night trembled with the beating of wings. But they would not descend on him.

Gently, his eyes still closed, he pressed his thumb against the thin bones in his wrists and felt the blood swell. Swell and subside. The beat orderly and strong.

His body lay at peace, all parts working smoothly. But it would not come to him, the vision, even though he knew it was so near, knew some presence was hovering outside in the night.

Burl

H<small>E</small> wished he could stay in the truck and keep a lookout for the haircutter from a warm place. But the truck had to be left on the farm road behind the trees if he wanted to keep his presence a secret. So there was no choice but to go to the house on foot. From there, in the shadows, he could keep a good lookout and not be seen himself. The only trouble was the cold. A swallow every now and then of the Jack Daniel's helped some, but he still hoped the haircutter would hurry up and come.

From where he was, standing at the side of the house behind some bushes, he could see the light go on in the bathroom and could even hear the water rushing up the pipes. Not much mystery about what was going on. There Lenora was, a shadow passing behind the shade, getting herself all ready for that haircutter. It burned him up, knowing she was up there making herself pretty for somebody else. Made his blood boil. Without even thinking about it he tightened his hand around the

gun and lifted it out of his pocket. Why didn't he
just charge into the house right now and let her
have it while she was getting ready for that lover of
hers?

But he held his ground under the trees, knowing
full well he wouldn't be satisfied to get her without
the haircutter. He was the one Burl wanted to
make suffer.

Still, just to give himself something to do, he
took the gun out of his pocket and pointed it upward at the lighted window. When the shadow
passed behind it again, he squeezed on the trigger
and said *Bang* to himself. But, hell, it was just a
game. Like a kid with a cowboy gun. Bang, bang,
you're dead.

He stuck the gun back in his pocket and moved
further under the trees. When he stumbled against
a big rock he sat on it and unscrewed the top of the
bottle.

All this waiting around for somebody to show up
so he could take his revenge brought to mind an
incident from his past that gave him satisfaction.
Twenty years before, on another winter day, he
had lain in wait for Jim Bob Haynes outside the
high school gym. He'd waited around the corner of
the building, keeping the door in sight, determined to take Jim Bob by surprise so he could get
what was coming to him. He'd had to wait for over
an hour, biding his time, waiting for basketball
practice to be over. Of course he was seen. Everybody but Jim Bob knew what was up, but nobody
was going to tell. They all knew what Jim Bob had
said. Everybody standing around outside the door
of fourth-period English had heard what he'd said:
that Burl Trotter's brains were in his balls, and his

balls were shriveled to the size of peas from all the bull riding he'd done. Some had laughed. Burl knew which ones.

Watching from his hiding place, Burl had taken note of the easy way Jim Bob came strolling out the door of the gym at four-thirty, swinging his basketball shoes by the laces and whistling through his teeth. Acting like he didn't have a care in the world. Probably thought he didn't. Jim Bob was a good six inches taller than Burl and figured he'd have the advantage in a fight. But if he thought this, Burl knew he was stupid, since Jim Bob was thin as a rake and Burl was built like a truck.

Burl, sitting on his rock and taking another swig of the whiskey, grinned, thinking about the way he had stepped out from his hiding place at the corner of the gym and said just two words—*Jim Bob!*— that had held Jim Bob rigid as a tree. And then Jim Bob had bent down and set his basketball shoes on the ground. Burl could remember just as plain —the way Jim Bob set his shoes on the ground as though they were something precious. He'd taken a quick look around too, like a hunted rabbit searching out a hole, but there wasn't a soul in sight.

Yet there was an audience—Burl was sure of this —to testify to the way Burl had beat the holy crud out of Jim Bob who did not stand one kind of a chance. He'd kicked him a few times even when he was down—that was when he got Jim Bob's front tooth—but he hadn't been sorry then and he wasn't sorry now. He hadn't cared that the incident got him expelled from school either. If he'd just dragged Jim Bob across the street and beat him up in somebody's yard, he might have gotten away with the whole thing. But no. He'd had to carry out his revenge right there on the school grounds. Burl never had been one to show common sense, and this was something he was proud of.

He wondered what Lenora would say if she pulled up the shade right then and saw him sitting on his rock, turning the gun around and around on his finger. She'd probably scream like a banshee.

While he was watching, his face turned up to the sky, the window suddenly went black. A minute more and the light came on in the bedroom. Following the action, Burl took his bottle and headed for the corner of the house under the girls' bedroom. From there he would be able to see the haircutter's Lincoln as soon as it turned into the driveway.

But when he slid off the rock everything under his feet seemed to dip, and the ground took a sudden tilt sideways. Maybe he'd had more of that Jack Daniel's than he'd realized. Holding tight to the bottle, his hand clamped around its neck, Burl felt like he was walking over a whole yardful of rocks. His feet slipped from under him and he dropped the bottle, grabbing wildly. For a moment his hands clutched a tree limb, but no sooner did he touch it than it snapped—the noise loud as a shot.

He lay sprawled on the ground, scarcely breathing, startled by the silence that followed the loud crack. Surely everybody in the house had heard that noise.

But when he lifted his head from the ground and looked up, he saw that the girls' window had remained dark. This was luck he hadn't expected, and he took heart.

There was his bottle too, lying intact beside his right knee. He seized it and cautiously sat up.

Sitting where he was, cross-legged, with the bottle between his thighs, he could see the driveway when he leaned sideways and that was all that mattered. He'd be bound to hear the car as it slowed, and would see the headlights picking out the trees. If he turned his head he knew he could see the light from the bedroom where Lenora waited for her sweetheart, but he kept his head where it was. He knew where to find Lenora, and she'd be there when he was ready. She wasn't going anyplace.

Adele

AGAINST her side Martha's breath rose and fell, and as she breathed her skin gave off the smell of soap. Adele rolled over and looked into Martha's face and wished she could wake her so they could whisper together under the covers. But she didn't. Not yet. She'd have to wait until her mother went to bed.

Now that Adele's eyes were used to the darkness she could see the crack in the plaster above her head that weaved up the wall like a snake moving toward the brown stain where the rain had gotten in through a weak place in the roof.

Around her the house breathed. A gentle straining of wood on wood and then the slow subsidence. It breathed very slowly, the sound hidden from any but the sharpest ears.

For a long time her mother cleaned the house, putting into cupboards all the things that had been misplaced, and Adele listened, soothed by the knowledge that her mother was moving through the house. Once—wasn't it true?—her mother's presence had filled the rooms and there had been nothing to be afraid of. As she lay there listening, she started making up the old, familiar story, the one she and Martha had told each other for so long.

Once upon a time there was a house, a log cabin set under trees, surrounded by woods and rolling pastures. When you opened the door of the house you saw there was only one room. In that single room the family lived and slept, never far from one another. At one side of the room the beds were lined up, four beds in a row, and on the other side under the windows where the morning sun streamed in, there was a table where they ate. One of the girls who lived in the house had long hair, the other short. They were nearly the same age and they loved each other and rarely quarreled. In the barn, not far from the house, there were many horses and because there were so many that could be sold for a lot of money, nobody in the family had to go away to work. All day the father and mother were at home exercising the horses and feeding them grain. When the two girls came home from school they took their ponies and galloped across the fields, and there was no special time they had to be back. In the barn every horse had its own saddle and bridle and blanket as well as a lead rope and feeding bucket. Hanging from nails, in a neat row, there were picks to clean out the horses' hooves. There were currycombs and dandy-brushes and sponges for giving the horses baths. Cans of oil and English saddle soap sat on shelves. Everything was always in its place and things were never lost.

The family had always lived in the house and they would never move.

In the bathroom there was the sound of running water—her mother filling the tub—and Adele listened, half asleep, knowing that her mother was leaning over the tub sprinkling bath salts into the water. Then she would take off her robe and carefully slip into the water. Adele could hear sloshing as her mother reached for the soap. After a long time there was a loud gurgle as her mother climbed from the water, and then Adele knew she was drying herself. Adele could not hear this but she could guess how her mother stood in front of the mirror shifting from one foot to the other, causing a soft spot in the floor to creak. Her father had said he would fix that board in the bathroom just as he said he would fill in the holes in the walls and paint every room. Then he would repair the roof so the rain couldn't seep in, and in the spring they would plow the ground for a vegetable garden. Under the windows roses and hyacinths would flower.

But now there were dark stains on the rugs and wind shook the windows and made them rattle. It was cold in the house where rain seeped through holes in the roof and made dangerous blotches on the ceilings of the rooms. Shadows moved in the corners. Bills piled up on the windowsill. Their mother's eyes rested on Adele and Martha, but she didn't truly see them. She only knew *There is a child eating its supper. There is a child of mine with her hair unbrushed.*

Adele and Martha lay under the covers, their breathing as shallow as that of a rabbit Adele had seen once, lying bloody at the side of the highway with its legs twitching.

Carefully she rolled away from Martha's side of the bed and, with her head on her elbow, listened to her heart beating against the sheet.

"Martha," she whispered, leaning over, brushing her lips against Martha's ear. "Wake up, Martha."

Martha lifted her hand and brushed at her ear the way she would to discourage a fly.

Adele shook Martha's shoulder. "You have to wake up, Martha. We have to get up."

She felt, under her hand, Martha come suddenly awake and put her arms around Adele's neck, wrapping her legs around Adele's waist the way she did when she was afraid or when she was pretending she was a monkey.

"What's the matter?"

"We have to go," she told Martha softly. "You know what I've been telling you? That sometime we would leave? We'd go down to Grandma's? Well, we have to go."

"It's nighttime, Adele. Why can't we go tomorrow?"

If they didn't leave they would have to come into the empty house again after school, and she was not sure she could do this again. Each day it became worse. But she wouldn't tell that to Martha. "We have to go tonight while nobody will know. Remember how it was at Grandma's when we slept in that bed right by hers? Remember how you could hear a bird singing, even in the middle of the night?"

"No," Martha said. "It's dark now, Adele."

"It won't be dark long if we get up now. By breakfast time we'll be there."

She was not certain this was true, but the trip seemed, in her memory, to be of that length.

Outside, just beyond their window, there was a loud cracking noise. Then a thud.

"What was that?" Martha said, clutching Adele again.

"It's not anything," she told Martha. But she knew this couldn't be true. There was something out there in the night as there had been something inside the house that afternoon.

"Put your clothes on," she said. "Warm clothes. Be very quiet."

She pushed back the covers and put her feet onto the cold floor. In front of the chest of drawers where she kept her clothes, she knelt, recognizing by feel her jeans and sweater. It seemed her hands knew just where to reach. In the darkness she pulled her gown over her head and reached her hands into the arms of her sweater. Now that they had started and she knew it would be only a matter of minutes until they would be able to shut the door of the house behind them, she felt almost happy. Soon they would be at Grandma's house. How surprised their grandma would be to see them when they opened the gate and came up the path. She hoped Grandma would be sitting on the porch so she could see them as soon as they arrived.

Of course Martha needed help. She couldn't find her underwear, she couldn't find her socks. Adele had to reach into the drawers carefully, finding clothes for Martha. She even had to pull Martha's sweater over her head, she was such a baby.

But she remembered everything. The fifteen dollars she had been saving. Their gloves and warm caps. Until somebody gave them a ride they would be outside in the cold and they had to be prepared.

When everything was done she took Martha's hand and opened the door. A crack of light showed under their mother's door so she put her finger to her lips, frowning at Martha to warn her although Martha nodded vigorously, showing she knew very well what Adele wanted her to do.

They slid past their mother's bedroom in their sneakers and carefully went down the stairs, sticking close to the railing where the boards wouldn't creak. Since their mother had forgotten to turn out the light in the living room, it was easy to pass through it. As Adele tiptoed toward the door she thought she heard her mother's voice call out. But instead of answering, she shut the door quickly behind them, took Martha's hand, and ran under the trees.

Jeff

Under the shadow of the trees two figures emerged. For a moment they hesitated, holding hands, then ran through the yard and down the driveway. Of course it was Adele and Martha. He wasn't at all surprised to see them. In fact, he half believed he'd expected them all along, had been waiting for them to appear.

He grabbed his coat and ran down the stairs so quickly that when he reached the road they hadn't gone very far. There they were just ahead, walking along the shoulder carefully the way they'd been taught.

For the second time that night he ran, his sneakers sending gravel down the bank to roll into the grass.

"Adele!" he called when he was near enough. "Wait. Adele!"

He saw the two figures clutch each other, and even in the darkness he could see how frightened their eyes were. He realized as they backed away that to them he was only a dark, looming shape, the embodiment of whatever it was that they were running away from.

"It's Jeff," he said, the word sounding odd to him. He had never liked saying his own name although it wasn't the name itself that he minded—that sound fitted between teeth and lip. It was only that the sound had no connection with him. *Jeff.* What did that mean? What was the connection between that sound and himself: those sneakers crunching on the gravel; that hand, big and raw-boned with the skin over the knuckles chapped, which he reached out to Adele? There was *something,* yes, some organizer of all the perceptions that came through ear and eye and hand, some presence that anyone could see when they looked into his eyes, and yet he could not attach that sound, *Jeff,* to what he knew.

"It's me," he said again to Adele, but she drew back, pulling Martha with her.

"No," she said. Her arm raised, she would have pushed him back with her hand. He could see that she was poised to run.

"Your brother Jeff," he said again. He had never before said those words, though he found that there was a formality in them that steadied him.

"I thought you were chasing us," Adele said. "You looked like something scary trying to catch us."

"No. I saw you go down the driveway. What do you think you're doing out here, heading down the road?"

"We're going to Grandma's," Martha told him. "By breakfast time we'll be there."

"In the middle of the night? How do you plan on getting there?"

"We'll get a ride," Adele told him. "Somebody will pick us up. We're going to hitchhike."

"You can't do that. Someone bad might pick you up. You can't trust strangers."

"We have to go," Adele said, holding back.

"Why?"

"Because."

"Because of what you saw in the house today?"

But he had spoken of this too soon. He could feel Adele pull away.

"We have to go to Grandma's."

"But it's night. Aren't you scared out here by yourselves?"

She wouldn't say it, but he knew what she was thinking. To go back was what scared her.

"We could get there by morning and Grandma'll be glad to see us."

"Listen. If you have to go I'll help you. Tomorrow I'll help you. But you can't go tonight. Tonight you can come back to my room. You can stay there with me tonight."

"In your bed?" Martha said.

"Scott's maybe. Scott isn't there."

He would coax them. He would be careful and gentle.

They would come back with him because he was their big brother and because the night was very dark and now that they had put their clothes on and had started down the road they would know, or at least Adele would know, that the rest of the way before them was very uncertain. When they got to the main highway they wouldn't even know which direction to take.

"Tomorrow," he said again. "I've got money and I can help you tomorrow. There're buses.

There are ways of going and I can take you to the
right place."

"All right," Martha said, easily decided. "Let's
do that, Adele. We can go to Jeff's tonight and go
to Grandma's in the morning."

Adele hesitated. He could tell she thought that
once they started they should keep going. Adele
was more like him than Scott or Martha were. She
had the same kind of eyes he did. He had seen it
before, the way Adele watched, the way she too
kept a secret person in her head.

Jeff put out his hand to Adele, his palm touching the sleeve of her jacket. But even then he did
not hold her with his fingers. She would either
come with him or she wouldn't. If it was meant
to happen, then she would come of her own free
will.

He looked away from her as he waited for her to
decide.

"Well, okay," she said behind him. "I guess we
can wait until morning. Only early. Before
Momma gets up."

"All right," he agreed. "I promise I'll help you."

He did not look back over his shoulder but he
could hear them, their footsteps light on the gravel.
They might have been small animals, moving
warily through the woods.

Not once would he look back, not once would he
take their hands and draw them with him. They
would come because they had to come, because the
way had been ordered.

They had to scramble to keep up with his long
stride. But he need not accommodate himself.
They would follow now wherever he took them.

In the room above the garage, he put another

log in the stove and watched Martha and Adele take off their gloves and caps and coats. They did not know what to do with their things, so he laid them over a chair. Martha and Adele stood side by side in his room, looking at the rock posters that covered the walls: The Who in concert, the Grateful Dead picked out in luminous letters on a black background.

"You could sit down," he told them, a sense of formality having descended on all three.

They sat on the edge of Scott's bed with their hands folded between their knees.

"You could pull off your shoes and lie down," he told them. "It's very late."

They were so obedient it struck him as being strange. They immediately bent over to untie their shoelaces and then they lay back carefully on the bed, their arms at their sides, their heads on the same pillow. He turned off all the lights but one. "Close your eyes," he told them. "You can't sleep with your eyes open."

Martha's eyes closed but almost immediately opened again.

"Do you know any stories? Could you tell us a story so we could go to sleep?"

"I don't know any stories."

"You must know something."

He looked around the room for printed material, but all there seemed to be were old issues of *Hustler*.

"I'll find something," he told them, suddenly remembering the Bible in the back of his underwear drawer. "If you shut your eyes I'll read you something."

Again they shut their eyes and he looked at their

faces, the skin so smooth and pure under the light from the lamp. He wanted to touch it with his fingers, to run his thumb across their lips, molding them gently into that upward lilt, that look of peace and joy.

The book of Revelation was his favorite and he turned to it, to the first page, and read about how John had come to his vision on the island of Patmos, and what he had seen. God Himself, standing among seven candlesticks. " 'His head and his hairs were white like wool, as white as snow; and his eyes were as a flame of fire; And his feet like unto fine brass, as if they burned in a furnace; and his voice as the sound of many waters. And he had in his right hand seven stars: and out of his mouth went a sharp twoedged sword: and his countenance was as the sun shineth in his strength. And when I saw him, I fell at his feet as dead. And he laid his right hand upon me, saying unto me, Fear not; I am the first and the last: I am he that liveth, and was dead; and, behold, I am alive for evermore, Amen; and have the keys of hell and of death.' "

They were asleep before he was finished. But he would wait awhile, watching them. He did not have to worry about Scott coming back. With two girls to entertain, Scott was going to be busy. So he could sit in the chair watching his sisters sleep as long as he liked. When the time came that he must get up and go to them, he would know it.

Scott

I<small>T</small> was beyond belief. That crazy Jeff disappearing like that. Going to the john and not coming back, like he'd fallen through the pipes. Leaving him stuck with not one but two hot little chicks, just ripe and waiting. One little push and there they'd be. All he'd have to do was reach up his hand and let the good juicy fall right in. And the crazy nut had to choose that minute to leave, to take a powder. He probably never went to the john at all.

It was like Jeff to leave the three of them sitting there waiting while they finished off the pizza, leaving him to keep the old conversational ball in the air. But after a time it got ridiculous. After so long you couldn't just keep on saying, "What's he *doing* back there? Fell in or something?"

After a while there wasn't any choice but to go to the men's room and look although it was stupid and made him feel dumb. What it made him feel, exactly, was he had a brother that ought to be locked up.

Naturally, when he opened the door of the men's room the place was empty as a whore's teat. But he looked everywhere anyway, even putting his head down and looking under all the doors. Like he thought Jeff might be standing on a toilet seat or hanging from the ceiling. With Jeff there was no possibility too far out. But Jeff wasn't there. Nowhere. Vanished. Who knew where? Scott hoped he'd fallen in the lake.

Now what was he going to do with *two* girls? he asked himself, standing in the middle of the empty men's room. And what was he going to tell them? That his brother was a crazy?

Which he was. Jeff was okay, the only brother he had, and sometimes Jeff was fun and perfectly all right. But the boy was off his head too. Face it. He'd known that for a long time, so it wasn't some piece of knowledge that descended on him as a surprise at the moment he stared at the dirty towel hanging from its roller in the empty room. It was information he was well acquainted with. But why did Jeff have to go off like that on this night, of all times?

"Oh, shit!" Scott said, driving his fist against his palm. "Why now?"

But he'd be damned if he'd be defeated. Not with two girls sitting there ripe for the taking. No one was going to beat him out of what could so easily be his.

When he walked back to the table he squared his shoulders, ready to take on anything.

"Ladies, my brother has walked out on us all. That or else he'll give some sewage plant employee a bad turn tomorrow morning. Don't be too hard on him, though. Keep in mind he's not but sixteen and a shy boy. Takes fright easy."

The girls looked up into his face and dutifully laughed, not knowing what else to do, but the girl Jeff had left stranded—the one named Karen—had a downcast look about the eyes. Naturally she was probably wondering if she was such a gross-out that not even a sixteen-year-old boy could stand to spend twenty minutes with her. Which would not do. *That* couldn't be allowed, that defeatist thinking, or else the whole evening would be a write-off. Might as well kiss it good-bye right there.

It was therefore necessary to take Karen by the elbow and pull her from her half-empty side of the booth, necessary to slide her in ahead of him onto the bench he was sharing with Amy. Now they were all squeezed together on the same bench, but that was to the good. He could get his arms around both girls at once. He could give Karen a little nudge with his leg and start her on the way to cheerfulness. Give the girl her confidence back.

"Well, honeys, it's me, for the duration. But I'm twice as cute as Jeff. You won't miss a thing as far as my brother goes. Not when you've got me."

There it came—the color—back into Karen's cheek. It made him feel better to see her cut her eyes sideways at him through her lashes.

I picked you all the time, honey, he let his eyes say back to her. *We got us some little special thing going here that not even your friend knows about.*

Pressing Karen's thigh with his, he turned his head to Amy and gave her the same message. *You know I picked you first, sweetheart, but we can't let your friend feel left out, now, can we?*

Oh, he was sitting pretty, truth to tell.

A wild scheme began hatching itself in his mind. Two! Why not? Never had he had two at once although there'd been a few times he and Jeff had traded off. First one, then the other. But never two at once. Excitement rose, swelling in his stomach. Hot damn! Two! He could be sucking off one while he was pumping away on the other. Why hadn't he thought of that before? All those opportunities passed by when he could have had this very thing, maybe. Why hadn't he? Well, because he was always with that crazy Jeff, that's why. Stuck together like Siamese twins. Always in a partnership it had never occurred to him to question. Might be the best thing that ever happened, Jeff going off like that. The beginning of an experience he had not dreamed of. Well, no. He *had* dreamed of it, more times than one. He just hadn't thought about trying to bring it about.

"What about us getting some beer and having some fun?" he said, giving half the sentence to Karen and the other half to Amy. Giving each of them a little something—wrapping his leg around Karen's, giving Amy's shoulder a slow, enticing rub with his thumb. "That okay?"

They consulted with each other across his chest while he teased them by blowing into their hair and making it fluff out.

It wasn't necessary for a word to pass between them. A look was sufficient.

"Why, sure, we can stay out a while longer," Amy said. The moment she spoke he rose from the bench and began bustling the two girls out of the Pizza Kitchen. No time for second thoughts. Time now to put on the action. Speed so fast they would have no moment to reconsider.

Charles

His wife was used to the strange hours he kept since for as long as she'd known him he never slept more than five hours a night. Sometimes even less. For years he had worried that this was an unhealthy pattern that would make him prematurely old since he would have used up his allotted time more rapidly than other people. But having consulted doctor after doctor he had finally been convinced that he was merely one of those rare people who did not need much sleep. There was certainly nothing to indicate there was anything wrong with him. On the contrary, he was usually in magnificent health. And he took pains to ensure this would continue, spending a fortune on vitamin pills of all colors and sizes. Some he took in the mornings, with breakfast. Others with dinner. And he believed in exercise. Laps up and down the pool at the Y. Tennis. For a man of his age—and what that was few knew—he was in remarkable shape. He should know since he observed others with an experienced, critical eye.

It had fascinated him from childhood—the rites necessary to keep the body youthful and desirable. How well he remembered himself as a child, sitting cross-legged on his mother's bedspread, the satin soft against his bare skin. He loved to watch her at her dressing table—the slow, orderly progression of creams, astringents, masks—seeing it all in a kind of languorous dream. The careful concern his mother had for every detail gave him pleasure. In fact, later he would realize that those hours spent sliding his legs slowly over the cool slickness of the bedspread in the high-ceilinged room where the ivy extended tendrils along the windows as he watched his mother in silence—the slapping of her fingers against her cheeks to bring out the color, the sliding of Kleenex after Kleenex from the square box she held in her lap—had been the most sensuous moments of his life.

He admired his mother's beauty as he admired his own. Yet this admiration was of an abstract kind. It was the machine he admired. The beauty of his skin, the symmetry of his face, the fleetness of his long, wiry legs. He would have admired the body he possessed even if it had belonged to someone else. He was modest and knew that the well-made elegance of his body did not come about because of any virtue on his part. It was merely another way he was lucky. He admired beauty wherever he saw it. In fact, he could have burst into spontaneous applause whenever a beautiful woman came into his shop. And to tend to beauty, to preserve its bloom as long as possible—this was his calling. Beautiful women who knew their own beauty did not arouse his sexual interest, however. More to his taste were those women who had potential beauty that they were unaware of.

He got the same kind of pleasure from showing these women what was possible as (though he supposed this was a strange thing to say) those who spent their lives saving other objects of beauty from ruin—the restorers of old houses or paintings or fine furniture—got from their work. But his art was more important and more satisfying. The women who flowered through his efforts were always grateful, and most fell a little in love with him.

The woman who was later to become his wife had come into his shop one day, a round-shouldered girl with a squint. Others would have said she was plain, even ugly, but he had penetrated the unpromising surface and could see, from the first, the classic beauty of the bone structure, the line of the lips. And how grateful she had been when the transformation was complete! He was used to admiration and even love from his clients, but there was something about this woman that moved him too—a dignity and reserve which he liked. She was never one of the gushy ones; it was only by looking into her eyes that he could tell what she felt. And he liked that—the secret held between them that didn't have to be put into words.

He had asked her to marry him and she had accepted although her parents disapproved of the marriage—disapproved of *him*. Oddly enough he had understood their disapproval and was in sympathy with it, a little. He was twelve years older than their daughter, and they had had higher ambitions for her than marrying a hairdresser in the town where she was a college student. But she had married him anyway.

Privately he had not expected the marriage to last long. Yet, to his surprise, his wife remained in love with him. Perhaps it was the difference in their ages that encouraged this almost adolescent admiration on her part. He was the first man who had seen her beauty, the first man to make love to her. And, if he said so himself, he was a good lover.

He was not unhappy living with his wife, and yet she bored him a little. It was not his nature to be faithful to one woman. So many women found him attractive, and he couldn't help responding. None of it was serious, really, and there was no harm done that he could see. Of course he didn't tell his wife about these other women. Why should he disturb her? There were times when he was nearly certain she knew, anyway. And there were other times when he was sure she knew nothing about his secret life. In any case she stayed with him and was, he believed, even happy.

Since it was late and his wife was asleep upstairs, he turned the volume of the stereo low though he knew she slept heavily, falling into sleep early and waking with the light. She would then go jogging for four miles before breakfast and have spent what seemed to him already a productive day before she went off to her job at the agency for social services when he was just getting out of bed.

However, his wife, who was such an energetic person, did not appreciate the pleasures of the night as he did. He reveled in the silence and the rich sense of time that the night provided. If he had been a creative person he would have written poetry in those long, quiet hours, or he would have worked contentedly, filling canvases with colored shapes.

As it was, he sometimes did nothing but sit drinking wine and listening to music. But what he liked doing best was using that peaceful time in the middle of the night to cook elaborate dishes. It wasn't that he was greedy, though good food was important to him. It was the challenge he liked. Preparing chicken Kiev or pouring salmon mousse into a mold, he forgot everything else.

Tonight he was absorbed in putting just the right amount of stuffing into the middle of a grape leaf and turning the ends carefully under. But when he straightened up for a moment to take a sip of Moselle, he was disturbed by a sense of depression. What was the reason? As he sipped wine he considered, looking down at the neat row of stuffed grape leaves. He'd told Lenora he would come out to the farmhouse that night.

The sinking sensation he felt when he remembered took him by surprise. Was he that tired of Lenora, already? He would not have thought so. The beauty of her face still moved him, and he was amused by her mind, which was both naive and full of every romantic cliché known to man. Yet she had a greater subtlety than he would have expected. If you could start at the very foundation and work up—like that man, the one who took a cockney English girl and turned her into a lady— then you might come out with a surprise in Lenora. Or then again, you might find that the shallow trashiness permeated the very depths of her soul and could not be rooted out. But whichever one it turned out to be would not matter since he had no intention of spending months of his life transforming Lenora Trotter into some suburban matron.

He would leave Lenora much as he had found her after having provided, he felt sure, the romance of her life. A sweet secret she might one day tell a grandchild. She would be disappointed, of course, when the affair was over, but she would quickly recover and her husband, who had moved out of the house in a rage, would be glad to make up. Indeed he'd have more respect for her than before—though he probably would not admit this —because his wife had captured and held for a while a handsome and desirable man. Even Lenora would think more highly of herself and would walk with a new confidence. Here she was, a woman who could break hearts. This happy outcome—so beneficial for everyone—would be even more likely to come about if he could end the affair in his own way. He would continue to declare his love for Lenora even while he told her, sadly, that their affair couldn't last. After all, they were both married and had other responsibilities to uphold. Though it would cause them pain—and they would be united in their suffering—they must give each other up for a higher ideal.

He well knew that Lenora would fall for this and even be deeply moved. How appealing she would find it—the sacrifice of individual happiness for the higher good.

But why, if he was still attracted to Lenora—and he believed he was—did he feel a reluctance to go to the farmhouse that night? Perhaps it was because the night was chilly and he didn't take pleasure in the five-mile drive. Perhaps he didn't want to stop the job he was doing.

His reluctance diminished, however, when he thought about how she would be waiting for him. Having employed all the fantasies that movies and country music had told her were conducive to a night of love (and this was how she would think of it, A NIGHT OF LOVE, shown in brilliant colors against a dark screen), she would be waiting for him wearing a sexy gown. There would be perfume sprayed into the air and the radio playing softly. Lenora, looking like a girl with that eager smile on her face, would be spread like a sacrifice all for him under the pink light that knocked him out every time he saw it. The perfect touch. A touch of such vulgarity that he could never have thought of it himself. For reasons that Lenora would never understand, the pink frilly lamp, the sexy gown, the perfume, would certainly have the desired effect on him. He did want to go to her after all. Nore, Nore, his little hillbilly whore.

Grace

THE sweat was just pouring off her when she suddenly opened her eyes. But for the longest time, even though she lay there looking directly at that window—could see it just as plain as plain—the room wouldn't fall into place. She kept trying to make it out to be one particular room, but it couldn't be the one she thought it was. When she first opened her eyes she was so sure she was in the old homeplace, in the house she'd been a little child in. Wasn't it funny how things seemed different at night than they did in the day? She kept looking at that window and thinking *There shouldn't be no window there*. But she could look at that window all night and it wouldn't move over where it was supposed to be.

And then all of a sudden she knew where she was. There was Virgil snoring away, lying flat on his back, which always made him snore the worst. "Go on, move over, Virgil," she told him, and dug her elbow in under his ribs so as to roll him over.

Seemed like she spent half her time these days trying to persuade Virgil to wake up or to move over. He sure wasn't much in the way of company.

And she could use a little company after that bad dream she'd had. What had that dream been about, anyway? Left her lying there in her own sweat and then slipped right out of her head. Her heart was pounding so hard that when she put her hand to her breast she could feel it knocking. Had to draw up her breath from some great depth, like lifting a full bucket from a well.

But then as she made her way to the bathroom, using a chair for support, sliding it along the floor in front of her, the dream or whatever it was came back to her.

Oh, lord, not *that* one again, she said to herself. That one was so scary. Not even any pictures in it like a regular dream. Only, every time, there she was, lying on her back in her bed—she kind of knew where she was only it wasn't clear—and her breath was stopped in her chest. First she would try to draw it in. That failing, she would try to push it out. But she couldn't force it out either. Her chest was plain stopped. Not in and not out. She knew, every time this dream came to her, that if she could just move one little finger she would be saved. Just one tiny little movement. So she would lie there straining and straining, trying to remember how to get her hand to move. But the effort it cost made her break out in sweat. It was just like putting her shoulder against a house and expecting to shove it across the ground. One little finger. One finger lifted an inch and the spell would be broken.

But every time it ended up the same way. Just when she knew she couldn't take another second of

it—her lungs were going to burst like two balloons
—her eyes would fly open and she would be able to
take in a long sweet breath of air.

What scared her so bad was the fear of what
would happen if one time her eyes didn't fly open
like that. If she couldn't get herself to move, even
so much as one little finger, why, she'd smother to
death. Lying right there beside Virgil and him not
knowing a thing. He'd wake up in the morning
and there she'd be, stretched out beside him stiff as
a broom handle. What a turn that'd give him. The
shock might carry him off too and they would
reach the pearly gates at practically the same time.
She'd grab him by the hand and say, "Get yourself
on in here, Virgil. You always were a slowpoke."

She pushed the chair all the way into the bathroom and positioned it while she eased onto the
toilet seat. Once down she was all right until she
had to get up again. And while she was down there,
sitting at her ease, she scolded herself. Here she
was, an old woman of seventy-nine. Just how much
longer was she planning on going, anyway? She'd
had her life, and all things said and done it'd been
a good life. Full of hard work and trials, but she
and Virgil had lived through it all—the bad times
and the good. So why was she so scared of being
taken? The good Lord was going to take her one
day soon, that was certain. And surely she was
ready to go. Her salvation had been bought by the
blood of the lamb and attested to. She didn't doubt
it.

Still, why did He have to scare her so bad before
He took her? Why did He have to make people
suffer so before they were allowed to approach the
throne of grace? That was a thing she never had

understood. Never would. The truth was the Lord wasn't always merciful. She would be scared to say that out loud, but to herself, in the dead of night, in her own bathroom, she'd admit it. Something was wrong with this old world that preachers wouldn't admit to.

Lenora

She knew she looked pretty with her hair fluffed over the pillow. The bath had done wonders. And she'd gone beyond being tired—a thing she'd noticed before. If she stayed awake past a certain point she wasn't sleepy any longer. The tiredness passed away and she felt lively, ready for anything. This would be a good time for Charles to come, right then when she was feeling so much better.

And yet she hoped he wouldn't come for a little while so she'd have time to imagine how it would be when he got there. She could picture his hands and lips touching her all over and could hear him say, "Oh, my beautiful girl, my pretty baby." She could have him say anything. "I can't live without you. We'll be together always." Together they would see the world—Paris, the Caribbean islands —wherever she had her heart set on going.

But daydreams were good only when he might arrive at any minute. Other times they just made her miss him more than ever—they put her in a terrible state of the blues. Even when Charles was with her, his warm body lying beside hers, there were times when his thoughts were a long way away. "What is it?" she would ask him, but he'd only shake his head and smile. He'd never tell her. And that made her blue, too. She would tell him anything, but he didn't feel the same way.

Once she thought she heard footsteps downstairs and called out, "Is that you?" her heart starting to pound. But it was just her imagination getting carried away. Nobody was coming up the stairs. It was still much too early—only midnight. She knew he wouldn't get away until later than that.

Nothing to do but wait.

After a while she took a bottle of perfume from the bedside table and sprayed it into the air, all around the bed. She knew Charles liked that, coming into a room where the air was full of perfume.

When she settled back down, though, what came into her head wasn't anything to do with Charles. For some reason she thought back to when she was in high school and going steady with Lawton Collins. That was when Lawton was a junior and she was a freshman. Lawton used to take her to the movies in his daddy's pickup, and on the way home he'd park in the dark stretch of road behind the old canning plant. It wasn't a popular place to park because the view, if you bothered to look, wasn't much. A bunch of dumpsters behind an old sagging mesh fence. Not that she and Lawton wasted much time viewing the scenery. She would never forget those kisses, her teeth and Lawton's coming together with a click, and how Lawton's

hands sweated when he pulled down the straps of
her bra and fastened his lips onto her breasts, making noises in the back of his throat like he was on
the point of strangling to death. She never would
let him go all the way, though holding him back
hadn't been easy. That had been the most exciting
thing—their struggles in the cab of the pickup. It
was the first for her, after all. Before Lawton she
hadn't known what kissing was.

Lawton had been crazy about her. She knew
that. Everybody did. All her friends were wild with
envy because there Lawton was, not only crazy
about her but good-looking to boot, and besides,
his daddy owned the only drugstore in town. Between Lawton and Burl nobody else would have
hesitated a minute.

But she hadn't cared. Burl had something that
drew her eyes like a magnet every time she saw him
pass by in his daddy's pickup or come into the
Dairy Queen, looking around the place like he
owned it. Partly it was his curly hair and broad
shoulders. But it was more too. The recklessness
that made Burl ride those bucking horses and the
bulls with humped shoulders appealed to her. She
had known, if others didn't, that Burl would take
her places she would not otherwise go. And he had.
He was restless the same way she was. It wasn't for
Burl—sitting around in one place all his life.

Whereas Lawton had never stirred from Pea
Ridge. In due time he took over his daddy's drugstore and built himself a nice-looking house out on
Highway 64. One of those ranch-type houses with a
long driveway going up to it. She'd passed it many
a time and thought, Well, you could be living in

that right now. Have a new car of your own every second year and no money worries. But she didn't really wish she'd married Lawton all the same.

Not that she exactly wanted the mess she had with Burl either. She did have to admit that. But life with Lawton wouldn't necessarily have been an improvement. Just different. Why couldn't there be something in between? Not constant moving around and debt and quarrels the way she had with Burl, and not being stuck in Pea Ridge all her life, either, the way she would have been with Lawton.

Of course Charles was something else. Life with Charles, if she could have that, might be perfect.

Her eyes closed. She seemed to be floating, her head under the lamp, her toes pointing to the foot of the bed. She was sitting in a bright room somewhere, a seaside place. Through the windows she could see the water, like a giant bedspread stretching all the way to the sky. A color like the iridescent green that black roosters exhibit in their tail feathers when the sun shines on them. She was sitting in that room wearing blue silk, a cool breeze against her legs. And a man, a handsome man, was coming through the door holding a drink in a tall glass, handing it to her. The glass was cold and little beads of water trailed down its sides. She was just reaching out her hand, so thirsty she couldn't wait to drink whatever was in the glass. She was sure it would be wonderful. Something cold that would taste like peaches. Her lips were all set, she was going to have it . . .

"Sleeping?" someone asked.

Her eyes opened and Charles filled them. He was standing in the doorway wearing his suede jacket,

the one that felt soft to touch, making him so good-
looking that shyness came over her and she pulled
the covers to her chin.

"Oh, no, I wasn't asleep. My eyes just closed a
minute."

He came into the room, closing the door softly
behind him. She liked it the way he always remembered things like that. He was such a gen-
tleman.

As usual when he was standing in front of her,
when he had actually arrived after all the waiting,
she felt a great urgency to talk and yet couldn't
decide what to say. She had always been such a
talker, ordinarily words fell from her mouth easily,
but Charles turned her quiet.

*Did you have any trouble getting out of the
house?* she considered asking, but it didn't sound
like the right kind of thing for her to say. *Gee, I'm
glad you've come* was also wrong somehow. It
might sound like a reproach, like she was scolding
him for making her wait so long. So she did nothing but smile. He did make her feel so young. She
could have gone back to being sixteen and
wouldn't have known the difference.

When he bent down and kissed her she could
smell the cologne he wore. If Burl ever wore
cologne she'd think he'd lost his mind, but she
liked Charles to wear it.

He undressed very quickly but also very neatly,
folding his clothes before he put them on the chair.
That was another thing that Burl would never
have done, but she liked it in Charles. He was like
a cat, so quick and slim and light on his feet.

When he threw back the covers and looked
down at her, touching her breasts through the

thinness of her gown, she felt a shiver go down her backbone as though a drop of cold water had fallen there. This was the very best part, the beginning, when he slid into bed beside her and she could see his skin glowing in the light of the lamp, when he loomed over her to run his hands over her breasts, her hips, easing up her gown inch by inch, watching her face to see it kindle, as she knew it did, with wanting him.

"Oh, sweetheart," she said. "You are the sweetest thing."

"My little whore," he whispered in her ear.

Burl

Aｆｔｅｒ a while he lay down by the rock, since he
could still see all he had to from there. He got
himself comfortable with his head resting on one
arm, good as a pillow, drinking whiskey and looking at the sky. From Lenora's bedroom the pink
light shone behind the shades. The whole place
looked like a whorehouse to him. She might just as
well have put a red light above the doorway.

It was dark in Adele and Martha's room. Poor
little things were sound asleep, all ignorant of what
was taking place around them. They probably
never heard a thing all those times the haircutter
had come there in the middle of the night. It was
dark over the garage too, but he noticed that the
boys' truck was gone so they were out somewhere,
carrying on the way boys did. Just as well they
were out of it all and didn't have to see the way
their mother was making a fool of herself.

He wasn't even cold any longer. The whiskey
had warmed him through and sent a curl of pure

heat right up his windpipe. Shoot, he could wait there all night if he had to, though he might be a little stiff when he tried to get up.

One thing he better remind himself to keep in mind. There was one thing that even in the excitement of the minute he better remember. When he went in that bedroom, gun in hand, and caught Lenora and the haircutter at it, right before his very eyes, he better keep in mind to shut the door behind him before he shot. One thing he didn't want was his two innocent little girls coming in on that mess. The blood all over the bed would be bad enough—that alone would give them bad dreams for the rest of their lives. But apart from that, they shouldn't see their own mother naked in bed with some stranger. He devoutly hoped they'd sleep through it all. What he wished he had was one of those silencers for his gun, like criminals had in the movies. Nothing but a little click and the person shot would keel over, dead before he knew what hit him. But he didn't know where you went about buying a silencer. You couldn't just walk into a sporting goods store and ask for one, he was pretty sure. Hell, the pistol wasn't even registered. Brought it with him from Cleveland. But he could have a whole houseful of guns and nobody would know the difference.

For a while he shut his eyes. No mistaking wheels on gravel or the sound of a car door opening. So he didn't worry about it. Just lay drinking whiskey and letting his mind drift. He thought once, when he opened his eyes, that he saw something move under the trees down by the driveway, but when he looked sharp he couldn't see anything. Probably it was just a shadow of some kind.

He settled back again and thought about horses. About throwing the saddle over the blanket and tightening the girth. Giving a good yank to make sure. Then swinging up—ball of his foot in the stirrup, reins easy. The feel of a good horse between his legs, his knees just naturally gripping, riding high the way he liked to do it. His legs and arms knowing that horse better than he knew himself. Perfect control. The little tightening of the thighs that meant lope, the slight lean forward that meant gallop. Cutting loose across a field, full tilt with the wind tearing at his hair. That was better than any woman, for his money. No woman that lived could give him that rush of pure freedom so he had to rise high in the saddle, throwing back his head, cutting loose with a yell.

Even there, lying on the cold ground with his arm going numb under his ear, he could have cried out in pleasure at the thought. Whatever else happened, that life waited for him somewhere. A person didn't hold a dream like that for as long as he had without it coming about sooner or later.

Excitement made him sit up forgetting all about where he was or why he'd been lying on the ground, when the headlights of a car cut along the driveway and rested on the trees. The engine was so smooth it didn't make more than a purring sound, but the noise of the car door opening was unmistakable.

For as long as it took for the car to come to a stop and the lights to go off, Burl just stared, unbelieving. It *was* the haircutter. Right up to that time, even though he'd been waiting around most of the afternoon and night for this particular man to come to the farmhouse, Burl hadn't believed it would really happen. He wasn't even altogether sure he'd believed in the haircutter's existence. But there was the car, and it sure wasn't some old wreck either. Even though he was no expert on cars, he could tell that this one had an expensive motor. It made the hackles rise on his neck just to hear that fine-tuned engine, and to see the strong beam of those headlights.

Whoever owned that car was a rich bastard who'd always had anything he wanted and probably thought he could go on the same way the rest of his life. It made Burl furious to think of the haircutter coming to the farmhouse like he owned the place. He'd probably never even considered that it was another man's house he was coming into, another man's wife he was about to climb in bed with. No. If he wanted something he took it. No thought given to right or wrong. But that haircutter was going to learn. Maybe the husbands of all the other women he'd fooled around with had been cowards. But this time he'd made a miscalculation. This time he'd gone too far and didn't even know it yet.

Burl fingered his gun, warming it up in his hand. There was plenty of time. He wanted to catch the haircutter in bed with his white butt sticking up in the air. He wanted to catch them hard at it. That was right where he wanted them: dead in the center of the bull's-eye.

Scott

He couldn't believe it. Felt like he'd died and gone to heaven. His wildest dreams wouldn't have provided him with a girl whose family had a little empty vacation house on the lake, and the key left in a holder under the eaves of the roof. Couldn't believe his luck in hustling the girls out of the Pizza Kitchen early enough to have the whole evening before them. He carried the beer—two big grocery sacks—under his arms, making sure they'd have plenty. He wasn't about to take any chances on ruining this opportunity. A chance like this might never come again.

Karen pushed open the door and there it was. A whole house to themselves, and nobody to bother them. He flicked on the lights, walked straight through the kitchen, and set the beer on the table. What he wanted to say was, Well, where's the bedroom? Where's the bed? Got no time to waste.

Instead he had to fool around a little. Had to

open up beers, had to see that the girls got some beer inside them right away.

"Have to chugalug the first two beers," he told them. "Those're the rules."

He tipped his head back and got busy on his own beer. Couldn't believe they'd do what he told them without a protest. But he could see them out of the corner of his eye drinking their beers faster than he was drinking his. They thought it was funny. He watched them, amazed. The first bottles were drunk just like that. "Don't lose your momentum," he told them, getting more bottles opened up fast. "Get another one going as soon as you set that bottle down."

Same thing with the next round. The girls' eyes were practically glazed by the end of that one. Both of them were leaning against the refrigerator laughing like someone just told them the funniest joke they ever heard, their eyes swimming like fish.

"I think we ought to go lie down awhile, don't you?" he told them, figuring it was okay to make his move. "That'll steady our heads."

They went with him like one cow following another to the pasture.

He gave an arm to each girl, marching them straight down the hallway. There had to be a bedroom down there somewhere, it only stood to reason. One thing was for sure: It was no time to stop and ask directions.

When he came to a door he tested it with the toe of his sneaker and it swung open. So he didn't even bother with the light. The important thing was that he could make out the shape of a bed, and he concentrated on getting them all to the edge of it. Then with one quick move he swung the girls around so the bed was behind them. When he felt the edge under his knees he pulled them all backwards, squealing, onto it.

Lying on the bed, his arms still around the girls' shoulders, he came to the ticklish part. He turned his head to kiss one girl while holding tight to the other and then reversed. Back and forth, he tried that a few times, but saw he'd have to shift into other, more aggressive moves. So he kissed Amy a good long one to hold her for a while and, turning to Karen, untied his shoe with one hand and pushed it off. On hands and knees, leaning over Karen, he got off the other shoe and pulled his belt through the loops. Now, down to essentials, he got busy on both pairs of breasts. But this was harder work. It required both hands to unbutton Amy's blouse and get her bra unhooked. Then he had to get Karen's tee shirt over her head and ditto with her bra. He was beginning to feel like somebody cramming two little kids into snowsuits and zipping them up. Tricky work.

But it was worth it. His hands and mouth were rewarded, going crazy with all those boobs. Little pointed ones of Amy's and full, strawberry-shaped ones of Karen's. Taking both hands then, slow, right down the main path, snapping open jeans with two quick yanks and sliding on down, under elastic, both hands coming into sweetness at the same time.

They were going to let him! Just like that. He was delirious with excitement and couldn't decide which one to go for first. Lucky thing he'd moved a couple of boxes of rubbers from his jacket to his jeans pockets when he was buying the beer. He figured he had enough to keep them going all night if he could hold out.

He decided to do Amy first, with a finger job for Karen. Made him feel like somebody in one of those photographs in a porno magazine—all those intertwining bodies joined in ways you had a hard time even figuring out.

That poor dummy Jeff. The dope had no idea what he was missing.

Jeff

Under the light of the lamp his sisters slept. He sat beside them, leaning over to study their faces in that state of peace that was close to perfection, although he could see that the thoughts they had were disturbing. Beneath their eyelids, thin and fine as silk, their eyes moved. Once Martha's mouth opened as though she would speak, but then she shut it again when she turned her head to one side.

He wanted to touch the skin of their foreheads and cheeks. He wanted to touch their lips with his thumbs and run his hands lightly over their faces like somebody making a piece of sculpture out of clay.

Who would have thought it would be so easy to bring the girls to the room with him and have them, now, on his bed, with their hair spread out over the pillow? If he had planned it, he would have failed. This was one thing he had learned.

But if he waited, if he listened to the interior voice that was as sure as the movement of blood through his body, then he moved with certainty. It was the way a person floats in a gently moving current of water—without thought or struggle. For a long time he had tried to sink into that current and let it move him in ways unheard of in that other world where he kidded around with the men in the garage or listened to Scott carry on about girls. He had long practiced tuning himself to that which was not a voice but was, nevertheless, certainty. God, was it? Moving through him?

When was the first time he had known that sense of himself settling into the depths? He'd been small, that was certain, and at first—for a long time —it had been the most terrifying thing he knew. Standing in the doorway of a kitchen—but in which house he no longer knew—he had looked into a room that changed in some mysterious way even as he watched. Objects did not move, colors did not change, and yet his connection with the room and the people in it was severed. He was cut off, afloat. Whatever it was that saw the wooden table, the woman walking back and forth between stove and cabinet, had come adrift and was consciousness only. Who was he?

Jeff, he told himself. *I am Jeff. That is my mother.*

But it wasn't true. There was no I. And without that there could be no mother.

There was no he.

There was only the wall. The stove. Hands held in front of eyes.

Jeff. He whispered it again.

But *Jeff* was word only. There was only the sound: *Jeffffff*.

There was the recording instrument still taking pictures, still hearing the sounds of footsteps crossing the kitchen floor. *Something* knew table, floor, wall. Knew the words, could identify objects. But he, Jeff, had lost all connection with these things.

He was lost.

And then, slowly, had returned. Like fitting one box into another he, Jeff, had slid back into the recording device that had never ceased its useless function.

The first time it happened, he had struggled against the division and had not wanted to be swept into the strange void, the place where he was not the small, individual speck *Jeff* but was set free from the self that lived like a squirrel in a cage, scrabbling in its minute boundaries. He had not known, then, that if he allowed himself to flow, to leave the confines of *I,* he would be swept into another state altogether, moving not through will nor decision but in another, deeper current that carried him in the direction he had to go. There was nothing without meaning, he knew at those times. Nothing could be that was not meant. All he had to do was to allow himself to be carried. He was instrument, only, of the force that ran like sap through trees, that swept the stars in their course.

Maybe what he knew at those times was what other people called God. The old saints, wanting to be swept far from earthly concerns and the sweaty sinfulness of the body, had wanted pure unity with God. The revelation of all mystery. He understood that perfectly. It was what he longed for too, as a parched tongue craves water.

Of course the mystery was terrifying. And yet he had known early that it was the only thing worthy of his most intense desire.

Yet, as far as he was able to go, there was a barrier that prevented him from going further. What the dying saw in the moment they leaped into the light was denied him. He had not seen God in the flesh.

Wind gusted around the corner of the garage with the force of powerful wings. He knew what it was, what rode in the wind. And he knew too he had only to allow it to take him up, to sweep him into itself.

Let me see. Let me know, he said to it. That one thing. Just that. *What can I do, Lord?*

It came to him as though in a voice but not through his ears as an ordinary voice would have been heard. Yet the word was clear. It came to him with the force of a great wind sweeping from far away. *Now,* it told him. *Now.*

And he got up from his chair and walked softly across the room to Scott's bed, bending to pick up the pillow which he took in both hands, carefully by the edges, holding it in front of him like an offering.

Lenora

EVERY time she was with Charles she felt as fresh and innocent as a virgin.

He crawled into bed beside her, and she pulled him on top of her, his skin so smooth, smelling so sweet, his hand soft on her body like no other man's she had ever known. Already her heart started to quicken. His head, looming between the lamp and her face, grew larger, blurred, as slowly he put his lips to hers, his tongue arching in her mouth. Reaching up for him she drew him down deeper and deeper, and she knew, then, she wasn't any girl after all, since no girl could be so greedy. Girls could never know what she knew. It took a lifetime of loving to find out.

She shut her eyes and her head slid off the pillow, her breasts pressed into his chest.

"Oh, sweetheart! Now!" she cried out to him. "Now!"

Adele and Burl

THERE was light in her eyes, too bright, the white sheet, the white pillow, the light too strong. Someone was kicking her. Someone was hitting. She was in bed with something thrashing; there was a fight going on in the bed right beside her.

Then she saw, against the light, bending in front of it, his eyes fixed on the whiteness, her brother Jeff. His eyes were closed and there was a look on his face as though he was listening to something a long way off. A look so strange that if she had not been sure, if she had not known her brother's ear, the shape of his nose, the dark-brown hair cut in a straight line across his neck, she would not have been sure that the face was his after all. He was smiling as though whatever he heard inside his head was a song, perhaps, of great beauty. And then he opened his eyes and looked down.

Now that he was inside the house, climbing the stairs, he felt good. He even puckered his lips as though he was thinking about whistling, though he knew better than to do it. Not when he had them right where he wanted them. The top of his head was still humming with all that whiskey he'd drunk, but he felt just fine. Now that things were under way he felt great. Why hadn't he done this before instead of spending all that time feeling sorry for himself? He ought to have come out to the farmhouse sooner, he saw that now. Action is what makes you feel good.

He held his hand cupped around the gun, his fingers bunching up the cloth of his jacket. He had to be careful not to let the gun bump against the stair railing, had to take every precaution. But he liked the feel of the gun in his pocket, knowing he was moments away from opening the bedroom door. Moments away from taking the gun from his pocket, slowly raising his arm, and taking aim.

Jeff was looking down at something white, held between his hands. He was gripping it so tightly that his knuckles, lying so near Adele's face, had turned pale.

Carefully she sat up.

There was a hand lying palm upward on the sheet nearly touching her leg. The palm was cupped as though to catch drops of rainwater. Adele knew it was Martha's hand lying open. One of her feet had come out of the covers too. One of her feet was in the cold, her toes slightly curled.

Without knowing why, Adele drew back from touching the hand although she knew it belonged to Martha, her sister whom she slept with every night. Many times she had waked and had to pull the covers up because Martha was such a restless sleeper. If Adele didn't stop her, Martha would kick all the blankets to the foot of the bed every time. Yet she did not pull the blanket over her sister's foot, where it stuck out in the cold.

She couldn't understand why Jeff was leaning forward, bending over something white that hid Martha's face, bending forward as though he was searching for something that had fallen off the head of the bed.

"Martha," Adele said, suddenly afraid. "Wake up, Martha."

When he took the door handle in his hand, it was just the way he knew it would be. He'd had his hand on that handle a hundred times in his mind. Holding his breath, he reached inside his pocket and slid his fingers around the gun. A grin came over his face and he knew he was enjoying himself. It felt to him just like something out of the movies, like he ought to have a camera pointing at his face.

But he couldn't stand there all night. And now that he was still, listening through the door, he could hear them in there, the bed giving on its springs, and somebody gasping for air. A rising scale going up to the high pitches.

He turned the handle, eased the door forward, and stepped inside the room.

The thing covering Martha's face was a pillow. She had known this from the beginning, as she had known from the beginning that it was her brother Jeff's hands holding so tightly to the edges of the pillow that his knuckles had turned pale.

But she hadn't wanted to know. As soon as she admitted the truth she would be terrified.

The word *Jeff* formed in her mouth—her breath gathered in her throat—but she would not say the word. Although she eased one foot to the floor and slid slowly to the edge of the bed, she made no sudden movement that would draw Jeff's attention to her, that might make him turn his head and look into her face.

But Jeff was intent on looking at something else. He leaned back on his thighs and his hands holding the pillow relaxed so the blood rushed into his knuckles and turned them pink. Gently he leaned forward to look over the edge of the pillow to what lay underneath. His lips parted. His breath held. Adele, unaware that she was doing it, leaned forward too.

Martha was lying with her eyes shut, her mouth open. She was very still, very beautiful, looking as though she might be yawning, just the corners of her lips upturned. Adele thought that perhaps she was yawning, that she was on the point of opening her eyes.

Jeff put the pillow carefully to one side and touched the corners of Martha's mouth with his thumbs. It seemed, then, that perhaps Martha was laughing.

Jeff's mouth opened, Adele could hear his indrawn breath. "Martha?" he said, bending low over Martha's face, just whispering the words. "Let me see too."

Adele, in that last moment, strained forward as

Jeff did. She reached out a hand to shake Martha by the shoulder, to wake her up . . .

There he was, just the way he'd planned it. He was standing in the doorway, blocking it, the same way John Wayne stood in front of all those skies, blocking the sunsets. But somehow that pink light got in his eyes and he couldn't take it all in. It was confusing, those bodies intertwined on top of the covers. Looked like they'd be cold, lying there without a stitch and not even a blanket to cover them.

Burl stood there, looking down at them in just the way he'd pictured it, but instead of them looking back at him, horror spreading itself over their faces, they didn't even look up. Made him feel like he'd gotten himself into the wrong room in a hotel. He felt silly, lifting the gun out of his pocket and pointing it. Maybe he was going to have to go over to the bed and yell at them before they'd take any notice. What he did do was pull the door forward and push it back, hard, so it slammed.

When they finally did look over their shoulders at him, the haircutter's mouth dropped open and a wild look came into his eyes.

What the haircutter did then—so fast Burl couldn't credit it—was to leap right off the bed and flatten himself on the floor. The haircutter had good reflexes. Burl would have to hand that to him. Never had he seen anybody move as fast as the haircutter did. And you had to take into consideration also how encumbered he was to start with by Lenora's arms and legs. It was something Burl could almost have admired.

Even more amazing, as soon as the haircutter touched the floor, he began disappearing. He went under the bed like a snake going down a hole. With his hands clasped against the crown of his head, the haircutter was giving Burl an anguished look and using his elbows to help propel himself backwards. His legs had already disappeared and the rest of him was going fast.

Burl saw there was no time to lose unless he wanted to go to the trouble of hauling the haircutter out from under the bed. So, not giving further thought to the matter, he steadied his hand and fired. There was a noise that shook his eardrums, and added to it was Lenora's scream.

All she could do was gasp and point to Martha's face. She had forgotten Jeff. But then she felt it. Jeff's head slowly turning to face her.

She was trapped by his eyes, which did not see her as Jeff, her brother, would have done. They were not the eyes of anyone she had ever known before. It was perfectly clear, when she looked into those eyes, what he was thinking. What he would do.

In an instant she was running for the door and grabbing the knob in her hand. She heard him, crossing the floor behind her, but she was already on the wooden stairs, running down them barefooted so that they rattled loudly behind her.

She crossed the yard and passed under the trees— the ground hard as stone under her feet—and then she was across the rickety boards of the porch and into the front door of the house. "Mother!" she cried. "Mother!"

There were noises coming from upstairs in the bedroom and she ran toward them, not knowing whether or not Jeff was behind her since she was too afraid to look. All she could do was to reach for the bedroom door which meant safety.

Wildly she turned the door handle, pushing frantically against the door with her shoulder, and suddenly it gave way and she was inside.

Sitting on the floor was a naked man with blood covering his arm. He was leaning against the wall keeping his fingers tight around the place where the blood trickled. Since it was the blood that held Adele's attention, it took her a long time to lift her eyes and see her father with a gun in his hand.

"Damn thing overfired," her father said plaintively, looking at the man leaning against the wall. "I had you. Would've got you right through the head and then this damn thing overfired."

On the bed her mother was kneeling, naked, her hands over her mouth, staring at the man where the blood ran between his fingers and fell in a trickle down his arm.

"It's only a flesh wound," the man said. "It's only my arm."

On the bed her mother moaned and said, "Oh, Charles, oh, Charles."

"Should've got this fool thing checked before I tried to use it," her father said. "Shouldn't've left anything to chance."

"Jeff killed Martha," Adele said, standing behind her father. "He put a pillow over her face and smothered her."

Her father opened the gun and blew down the

barrel. "I had it all worked out. I been waiting around here since afternoon freezing myself to death and then this thing overfired."

Her mother was watching the man with the hurt arm.

"Martha's dead," Adele said again. "Did you hear what I said?"

Her father turned around. "Hey, you're not supposed to be in here, Adele," he told her.

She had to tell them all over again what it was she had to say.

Charles

Of course he thought he was going to be killed in that ridiculous way, lying naked on the floor in his own helplessness. He should have expected something like that, he realized later, since he knew something about the type of man Burl was—one of those country bullies. Something had warned him. He'd felt a distinct foreboding when he drove to the farmhouse that night. But he had set his fears aside. He'd supposed Burl had found himself another woman by now and wouldn't be brooding, still, over Lenora.

But he should have known. That type did brood. Their manhood was challenged by a wife's infidelity, and they didn't have any better ideas about righting a wrong than by blowing somebody's brains out. And if he'd gotten himself killed it would have been no more than he deserved for allowing himself to get involved with a person like Lenora.

Burl's incompetence was all that had saved him.

He'd really thought, lying there on the cold floor and trying to find protection under the bed, that he would probably die that night in a way both messy and embarrassing. It would have been beneath his dignity to die that way, although at the moment he was lying on the floor with his hands over his head, he was thinking about neither the mess nor the embarrassment. At that time all that engaged his attention was fear. Not that he blamed himself for being afraid. Anyone else in those circumstances would have been afraid too. There was nothing like being naked and unarmed to put you in a fairly extreme state of fear when you were confronted by someone clothed and with a gun.

Considering everything, he had gotten off lightly. And he was well aware of this even as he carefully got to his feet and stood for a few seconds letting his head clear. The final indignity would be to faint because of the loss of a little blood. Not that there was anyone left in the room who might have seen him if he had fainted. They had all gone running off with the child who had come in, talking something about Martha being smothered under a pillow. Probably the child had waked suddenly in the middle of the night, heard strange noises, and taken fright. He didn't believe anyone had died. It was just a child's story.

In the bathroom he washed his arm and saw that blood was still trickling from the wound, but it had subsided. He was in no danger of bleeding to death. The wound was only superficial, but he would have to see a doctor.

Wrapping a washcloth around his arm, he went to the bedroom to dress. Now that his arm had begun to hurt he was surprised at how painful it was, although in some ways he was grateful for the pain. It kept his mind on what he had to do.

Already it was clear to him that he didn't want the police investigating what had happened. Nor could he bring any kind of charges against Burl. What he wanted was to be allowed to escape without any publicity. He would take the responsibility himself, telling his doctor that he had been cleaning his gun when it had accidentally gone off. Since he did keep a pistol, one legally registered, this story should raise no questions. He saw no reason why his doctor would want to see the gun that had been involved, or the bullet that had passed through his arm.

But, since Burl's gun was lying on the bed where he'd dropped it when he'd followed the child, Charles picked it up and put it in his pocket. All contingencies would be covered. And the next time he would be more careful about the woman he picked. No more Lenoras. That was finished.

Grace

I⊤ seemed like it could have been a better day to
put that poor precious lamb in the ground. Not a
day with a cruel wind whipping up and the sky so
dark. It was pitiful, the way the crowd shivered
around that little white box, and she was glad that
dark hole in the ground was covered over so she
didn't have to see it. Such a bad place to have to
leave a child.

More people had come to the funeral than she
would have imagined. Bonnie and Dell and the
MacPhersons who lived down the road. They had
known Burl since he was a baby. And she was
pleased to see that most of the members of the Mt.
Judah Baptist had turned out, coming because they
had respect for her and Virgil. Most of them didn't
know Burl or Lenora well. And of course there
were the kinfolks on both sides. Those she'd expected.

Her heart went out to Burl and Lenora, standing side by side, so bowed down with their trou-

bles. It was terrible enough to lose a child, but so much more heartbreaking to lose one the way they had. The poor boy had lost his mind and nobody even knew it.

Jeff had always been her favorite, though she had a special feeling for every one of them. But something about Jeff had always touched her especially: that sad, lost look on his face. She remembered it so well. Even when he was a little boy he was a quiet child. She hardly ever remembered him laughing. He'd had a hard time. She knew that. Lenora had him just after that move to Cleveland, and then when he still wasn't any more than a baby, they'd taken off and moved again.

It was the beginning of their troubles—she'd attest to that—when Burl and Lenora left their people and went up North to live among strangers. Things had turned bad on them from that time on. They'd had trouble over money and trouble over jobs, and nobody up there could help them over the hard times.

Jeff always was a child who noticed things. When she sat in the shade in the cool of the day, worn to the bone, it was Jeff who used to climb up on her knee and put his hand on her cheek. "Do you feel bad, Granny?" he would say.

On the night the terrible thing happened, Jeff was close to her heart. Somehow he had wanted her to save him, reaching out in the time of his extremity for his old granny. He had weighed on her spirit that whole evening. That was what she told Virgil later, after they got the phone call. She told Virgil that her heart had been troubled that night, heavy as lead, and she'd known it was Jeff who needed her. But she'd failed him.

Oh, she had felt the pain he was going through, had rocked it back and forth in her heart, but what could she do except take her troubles to the Lord? And why He had turned a deaf ear to her prayers she couldn't know. He must have His reasons. She had prayed as hard as she knew how, nearly groaning with the travail she felt. But it hadn't been enough.

Now, looking back, she understood it all in a way she couldn't have at the time. Even that spell she had in the middle of the night, that bad dream about not being able to breathe, was just what poor little Martha was having to endure. The poor child, being smothered to death under a pillow. It was more than her old heart could take. There were some things you just couldn't allow yourself to dwell on, because if you did you'd be as bad off as Jeff. Not that the poor boy could help it.

It brought tears to her eyes to think of Jeff locked up in that place. In that home or whatever they called it. Whatever he'd done he hadn't meant to do it. She was as sure of that as she was of her own name. He wouldn't any more hurt his little sister when he was himself than he'd go jump off a cliff. Such a good, sweet boy, and nothing would ever get her to change her mind on that. Never would she find it in her heart to blame Jeff.

Reaching out for support, she put her hand on Adele's shoulder. Adele was such a comfort the way she stood there so straight, taking it all so well. Her face pale and set. Maybe it was harder on Adele than it was on any of the rest of them. Adele had been such a little mother to Martha. It was a treat the way those two had played so well together. Why, she'd hardly ever heard them fight the way sisters generally did. They got along real well, playing with their dolls and having their tea parties. Adele didn't know it now, but she'd never get over this loss. Nobody could ever take the place of a sister.

She squeezed Adele's shoulder, and even through her coat she could feel those thin bones. Adele turned her face up to hers. Not a tear. She was so brave and good. "Come over here to Granny," she told Adele, pulling her over so she could warm her. But holding Adele was about like holding a stick. "Honey, we have to have faith in the Lord," she told her, pulling her close. "Not a sparrow falls to the ground but He knows."

Adele just stood there holding her shiny purse between her hands, too young to have an understanding of God's will, or to know the comfort of leaning in His arms. But she did seem to be giving her attention to what Brother Powell was saying, going fast through the service. He was in Corinthians somewhere—she could attest to that—but not where, in her own opinion, he ought to be. What he should be preaching on was First Corinthians 15:51–52: *Behold, I shew you a mystery; We shall not all sleep, but we shall all be changed, In a moment, in the twinkling of an eye, at the last trump: for the trumpet shall sound, and the dead shall be raised.* That was a part of the Bible that had always given her heart, but Brother Powell was wandering around somewhere else, talking something about light and darkness.

" 'For God, who commanded the light to shine out of darkness, hath shined in our hearts, to give the light of the knowledge of the glory of God in the face of Jesus Christ. . . . We are troubled on every side, yet not distressed; we are perplexed, but not in despair; persecuted, but not forsaken; cast down, but not destroyed.' " In her opinion this put a better face on the whole thing than anybody could feel easy with. The trouble on every side she could agree with, but it seemed like there was plenty to be distressed about too.

The truth was that Brother Powell, who was a young man and inexperienced, was having a hard time over this funeral, though anybody else might have trouble over it too. It just tore your heart, having to put a child into the ground. It wasn't right to put a child into the ground beside her grandmas and grandpas and uncles and aunts, most of them having lived good long lives. She never would understand how He could take such precious little ones. It was cruel. The world was a cruel, cruel place.

Martha had been so pretty with her curly blond hair. The prettiest one of Burl and Lenora's children.

She swayed back and forth in her grief, holding tight on to Adele. When she used up the handkerchief she had, Virgil handed over his, a big one the size of a table napkin. It was a comfort to put her face down in it and let go.

Adele

If only she hadn't turned back that night when she and Martha tried to run away. Again and again she went back to that time on the road when she'd held Martha's hand. The time when they were on their way to Grandma's house. If only she hadn't listened to Jeff.

She'd *known* they should leave. They had started, were on the road, holding each other's hands, on their way to a place of safety. And none of it had done any good. If only she had clutched Martha's hand so tightly she couldn't pull loose, and they had run, not stopping until they had come to the highway where someone would have seen them and stopped.

If she had done the thing she knew she should, then Martha would still be alive. They could play the ranch game in the corners of the house and Martha would still lie beside her in bed, her hair fanning over the pillow. They would be the two sisters, one with long hair and one with short.

Sitting on a stool in the corner of her grand-mother's dining room, Adele watched the people leaning over the table to help themselves to fried chicken and ham and fruit salad. If they had known Martha as she had, then they wouldn't want to eat anything. Their stomachs would feel as shriveled as hers did. She hated those people, eating fried chicken and talking, even laughing, as though it was an ordinary day. Her grandmother said it was a good idea for people to come to the house after someone had died. It gave the family something to do—to feed all those people and pour coffee in their cups. It took your mind off your grief, so her grandmother said, to think about other people and their needs for a little while. But it did not take her mind from her grief to see those other people enjoying themselves.

Adele watched her grandmother walking heavily between dining room and kitchen, carrying tea-spoons and bowls of sugar, refusing to let anybody else help. She was an old woman with a dress gone shiny in the seat from all those hours of sitting on church pews, so old her legs were marked with purple bulges where the veins strained against the confines of skin.

Before, when Adele visited in the summers, her grandmother hadn't seemed old. She was the first one out of bed, before daylight, and her solid tread, which caused the floorboards to tremble as she walked between table and stove, made Adele feel safe. When she and Martha ran into the kitchen their grandmother took time to hold them on her lap, calling them her little lap babies and asking them to give their old granny some sugar. It was

like sitting on a throne, sitting high on her grandmother's knee.

This time, although her grandmother still ran
her fingers through Adele's hair and told her she
was Granny's girl, there was a faraway look in her
eyes. She had to take little pills, now, for her heart.

The house too had changed since Adele saw it
last. The rooms had grown smaller in that time
and seemed more crowded with furniture. There
was a musty smell like old quilts that have lain a
long time in trunks, and stale air was trapped in
the cushions of the mohair sofa and in the lace
curtains yellowing at the windows.

Not even the outside of the house looked the
same. The two big cedar trees growing on either
side of the porch seemed to have grown gigantic,
and the house looked shrunken under them. Now,
in early winter, the leaves had fallen from the
other trees, but there under the cedars it was shady
and cold.

If Martha had been with her, Adele probably
wouldn't have noticed how old their grandmother
had gotten or how gloomy the house was. The two
of them would have sat cross-legged in front of the
picture hanging above the sideboard and made up
stories about the boy who was leading a cow down
a lane past a house with a thatched roof and roses
growing along the wall.

When night fell and they went to bed it would
be in the heavy walnut one carved with a ram's
head. They would reach their fingers above their
heads and trace along the ram's horns. Over them,
if it was a cool night, their great-granny's Star of
Texas quilt would be spread and they could run

their fingers over those troughs and ridges, along those patterns like mazes that had no end and no beginning and that made the quilt into a complex world of its own.

But now she was alone. The house was full of people but she was alone in the corner sitting on the tall stool, her heels pressing against the rungs. There was nothing to do but watch the clock sitting on the sideboard and wait for the hands to move.

"You'd better eat something," her mother said, holding out a heaped plate. "Aren't you hungry?"

She shook her head and stayed where she was, on her stool. Soon her mother went away again, still carrying the plate.

The minute hand of the clock had moved three small spaces. What a weight it carried! Hours of ordinary time had passed while the minute hand moved between one o'clock and five past. Adele turned her back on the clock. She wouldn't look at it. She wouldn't look until the shadows of the cedar trees started lengthening over the ground showing that time had passed for sure.

But what could she do while this was happening?

If Martha had been sitting there with her, they would have played the guessing game. She would have held Martha's hand in hers, opening out the palm like a writing tablet, and moving one finger across Martha's heart line and the line that predicted happiness, she would start writing a word, letter by letter. *S,* she would write over Martha's palm, and Martha would know instantly, even before she finished making the letter, that it was *saddle* she would write. They hardly ever got past the second letter when they played the guessing game because they knew each other so well. Their minds were that much alike.

Martha, the only sister she would have in this world, the only one who could ever be blood of her blood.

Lenora

ALL the time she was carrying cups of coffee to her kinfolks and passing around the tray of fried chicken her thoughts were elsewhere.

There she was again sitting on the edge of the bed in that room above the garage, rocking her baby on her lap for the very last time. Kissing Martha's pale cheeks and holding her close. Once or twice she was sure she saw Martha's eyelashes tremble, so she caught her breath and bent her head ready to watch Martha's eyes suddenly spring open.

"Wake up, honey," she kept saying to her. "Open your eyes, precious lamb."

She didn't know what she was saying, rocking Martha in her arms. There was just Martha and her shut off from everything else in the world, the way it had been when she'd cradled a nursing baby close.

And then she'd lifted her head and seen Jeff, holding his elbows in his hands and swaying back and forth in his chair. He hadn't been on her mind at all, not when she came in the room and saw her baby lying so pale and still on the bed.

"Jeff," she said to him then. "Jeff."

He looked up but she wasn't sure he saw her, there was such a faraway look in his eyes. It was like a high fever, that wildness she could see there. For a split second she felt it too—excitement, danger, joy pounding in the crown of her head. She caught her breath, recognizing the closest thing she knew to his state. Out of her mind in Charles's arms. Taken over, both of them, shaken in the power so even their names were lost.

"Jeffy," she cried, afraid. But she could tell he was swept too far out even to hear her.

So she hadn't gone to him, had never held his head against her breasts telling him he was still her boy. It was Martha she went on cradling, rocking back and forth so Martha's heels slid lazily across the sheet. Rocked the child she couldn't warm again no matter how tightly she held, and failed the other one, leaving him alone and uncomforted even though he was her child too.

Burl

I⊤ came to him the day of the funeral when he was standing beside Martha's little casket heaped over with flowers, surrounded by the faces of all those he'd known when he was just a boy. His brother Frank for one, turning the brim of his hat around in his fingers—Frank nearly bald and with his ears turning red in that cold wind, but standing beside the grave as solid as a post. Burl was so touched by all those mournful faces that he could have kissed every one of them right there in the middle of the service. It affected him powerfully to see that he and Lenora hadn't been forgotten in spite of the long time they'd been away. Pea Ridge was still home the way no other place could ever be.

Caught up in what he was feeling, Burl took Lenora's hand and squeezed it so hard she winced. He longed to tell her that everything was going to be all right—from that very moment their lives were going to change. She'd see. The people who

loved them were just like a wall to lean against.
There they were, every last one of them giving
support.

Later on, after the funeral, while they were eating dinner, Burl asked his daddy and Frank about
houses to rent.

"Thinking about coming back home, are you?"
his daddy said.

"I don't see no reason to go back. Nothing but
bad memories up there."

"I didn't see a reason for you to go off to start
with," his daddy said. "Only you had to get it out
of your system, I reckon."

"If you're looking for a house," Frank told him,
"you might look into the old Springer place. They
got that up for sale and hadn't sold it yet. Probably
rent it cheap. You know the one I'm talking about?
Out on Route Three?"

"Hell, Frank, I grew up here, didn't I? You
think I've forgot every single thing I ever knew?"

He could find the old Springer place blindfolded
if he had to. He'd hunted rabbits out that way lots
of times; old man Springer had one time sicced his
dog on Burl before he recognized who it was.

Now that Frank had put the idea in his head,
Burl was in a fever to go have a look at the house.
Didn't say a word to anybody. Just left his dirty
plate in the kitchen sink and headed out the back
door. On a day like that nobody was going to question his movements anyway since he had every
right to go off and grieve by himself if he felt like
it.

All it took was getting in the truck and driving
out of the yard to make him feel about one hundred percent better than he had for days. Every

stretch of woods he came to held some memory for him. Why, he'd spent years of his life walking that land and hunting that land and there wasn't anything he didn't know about it.

A bumpy road took him under the cedar trees to the old Springer place. There it sat, the house on a rise with two big maple trees growing in front, and behind the house and to the side a strong-looking barn standing. There was a stock pond visible in the distance and woods beyond that.

Burl slid out of the cab of the truck and walked up to the house. Locked, but he could see enough through the windows. Of course it needed painting and papering and fixing up, but that was fine with him. Working on the house would give him and Lenora something to do while they worked off the worst of their grief. It would fix up real well too.

When he walked around to the back, he was pleased to see there was a good level place that caught the south sun. Perfect place for a garden. In that sheltered place they'd be able to start English peas and spinach as early as February. And farther down, along the slope, would be ideal for peach trees.

Even the barn was everything he could hope for. Four horse stalls, and built onto the west wall was a house for chickens with roosts and laying boxes.

It was the place for them; he was sure of it. The whole thing maybe preordained. In this house they would be a family again, all working together and happy.

First off he'd get Adele the pony she'd always wanted, and that would cheer her up considerably. Since they'd be living where there was good grazing for horses most of the year, there wasn't any reason why they couldn't have several. He could just see them—racing across a green pasture with tails flying.

A job would turn up at the Daisy gun factory or in a lumber mill. He was bound to get a job since everything had worked together to bring them back down there again. Back home.

The very same day they put his little girl in the ground turned out to be the day their lives turned around and headed into the sun. The perfection of it all just took his breath away.

Scott

Sure, he knew all along Jeff was an oddball, but it came as a total shock he was loony-bin crazy. It didn't have to turn out that way. He'd take a bet on it. If Jeff hadn't gone hightailing it home that night when all hell broke loose, it would've been okay. If he'd come on out to that house on the lake with those two girls, he wouldn't have had any time to lose his mind. Those two would've kept him on the hop. After being with them, Jeff would've fallen into a sleep as sweet as a baby's. He was sure of it. And there would've been plenty for both of them too. So it was really bad luck Jeff had gone home that night.

Something must've snapped in his brain and left poor old Jeff swinging at the end of the string. It was the only explanation he could think of because Jeff sure hadn't seemed *that* crazy when he left the Pizza Kitchen. Peculiar, all right. Jeff was all the time doing something you wouldn't expect. But not *that* far-out. Not freaked out completely so he'd go home and put a pillow over his own sister's face and smother her to death. It filled him with disgust just to think about it. Embarrassing too. That was the kind of brother he was landed with for life. A crazy murderer.

The one time he went to that place where Jeff had gotten himself shut up, it made him break out in goose bumps. Creepy place where people either sat staring into space as still as so many rocks or else were pacing up and down moaning and taking on. He was about ready to freak out himself before he finally found Jeff sitting over in a corner. Staring at the wall, looked like. Told him, "Hi, buddy. How's it going?" Jeff didn't even flick an eyelash. Didn't even seem to hear.

It felt pretty strange to be sitting there trying to talk to a person who'd turned into a post. Made him feel foolish. It was hard work trying to think up something to say to somebody who was about as lively as a tombstone.

Finally he said, "You know those girls, Jeff? The ones you walked out on that night? Well, I'm here to tell you they were something else again. I had both of them to entertain. Nearly killed me, buddy boy."

But Jeff just stared straight ahead. Talking to a chair would have been just as easy. Well, he knew when he'd had enough. He had better things to do than sit around all day trying to think of something to say to somebody who wasn't even listening. It was depressing. Stuff like that was just more than he could take

Sure, he felt bad about Jeff, but what could he do? He wasn't any doctor and he sure wasn't any saint. And in his present state doctors or saints were all that Jeff could use. So after a few minutes he left that place like there was a witch chasing him. Didn't get any farther than the first bar he came to. Ducked in there and laid one on it took two days to recover from.

But he'd done his duty. He did go to see his crazy brother, and he came all the way down to Arkansas for the funeral. Even lay around there for a couple of days afterwards, though he had nothing whatsoever to do. Long before that he was sick of the entire thing.

Came as a shock to find out the rest of them were intending to *stay* down there. Not that there was anything to prevent them moving to that tick-infested part of the country if they wanted to. But not this kid. No, sirree. He was getting out of there bright and early, and he wouldn't breathe easy till that car of his was gunning down the straight and open, burning up the miles.

He was heading back to his own particular happy hunting ground so fast it'd burn your eyeballs black. He knew what was good for him and what he wanted out of this life, and staying down there sitting on his ass sure wasn't it.

APRIL

APRIL

Burl

Every time he turned off the road and went up the driveway to the house he felt his spirits rise. Now it was April and there was green everywhere. The maple leaves were still fuzzy, but up North there would still be snow on the ground. The wind would be raw, the sky cloudy. It made him feel smug, having escaped all that.

When he got home from the mill, he didn't even go inside the house. Instead he went straight to whatever job he had under way. Right now he was working his way around the pasture, resetting fence posts and tightening the barbed wire. When he finished with the pasture, he'd get going on the porch. He was planning on rebuilding the whole thing. Putting down new floorboards—everything. And when that was done he'd repaint the house. Nothing would help the looks of the place more than that. While he fed logs into the saw at the mill, he debated what color he ought to paint the house. Blue was what he first fixed on. But then he thought blue might be too dark. Kind of depressing. Yellow, maybe. Or barn-red. That was a cheerful color and would show up for a long distance. But it was hard to decide, and Lenora wouldn't help him out. "I don't care what you paint it" was all she'd tell him.

As he came to a stop behind the house he could see Adele down at the foot of the pasture, lying in the sunshine, watching that pony of hers graze. He waved, but she had her head turned away. No eyes for anything these days but that horse.

It tickled him to see her pleasure. Nothing had given him more satisfaction than buying that pony —one promise he'd managed to keep.

One of the best moments of his life, truth to tell: opening the back of that horse trailer and leading Shawnee out. Telling Adele, "Well, here she is, honey. All yours."

Of course Adele was crazy over Shawnee. Every afternoon he'd see her out in the pasture, riding Shawnee around or, more likely, just *looking* at her. Adele was so overcome at having a horse that half the time she couldn't bring herself to ride it. Just like somebody with a new car, worrying about every little speck of dust that fell. He told Adele she didn't have to worry about Shawnee. She couldn't hurt Shawnee by riding her around the pasture or taking her on the trail to the woods. Horses needed exercise. They liked to be ridden. But Adele was so protective. He'd take a bet, though, that by summertime they wouldn't be able to get her off Shawnee's back. She'd probably be demanding to eat her supper up there. One thing he could tell for sure: Adele was going to be one hell of a rider. A natural seat. And that was something you either had or you didn't. A gift, the way some people could pick out anything on a piano.

He was glad to say that Adele wasn't pining over Martha the way he thought she might. Naturally Adele hadn't *forgotten* Martha, but she never mentioned her. She seemed to have put all that out of her mind, and of course that was the way it should be. There was no use dwelling on the past. And Adele was just a happy little girl, growing up fast the way they all did.

Ever since they'd moved, things had worked out the way he knew they would. Adele had her pony. He had a job. Lenora had gotten work without any trouble. The business with the haircutter was finished and done with, and they had turned over a new leaf in their lives. They were going to be happier than they'd ever been before; some little voice inside his head assured him of this and he believed it.

Just getting back to the house every afternoon made him feel good. By the time he turned into the driveway he had the hours until dark all planned out; nothing gave him greater pleasure than the feeling that he was restoring order. If he worked every afternoon like that, as hard as he knew how, pretty soon they'd have a showplace out there. As he kept telling Lenora, it was going to look like something straight out of *House and Garden.*

Adele

SHE leaned against the slats along the side of the stall, resting her arm and chin on the top board so she could watch Shawnee, standing on the diagonal, flicking her tail lazily back and forth to discourage the flies that were already, in April, hovering over the feeding bin.

Twice a day Shawnee ate a scoop and a half of trim and a quarter of a bale of hay. Once a day her stall had to be cleaned and fresh water set inside in a bucket. Adele knew she was supposed to ride Shawnee, to give her exercise, to enjoy herself holding tightly to Shawnee's withers while she galloped across the scrubby pasture where the prickly pear waxed, sending its buds along the tough green stalk like rosy fingers.

But Adele just stood at the edge of the stall watching Shawnee's tail flick back and forth across her hocks. She studied the way whiskers sprouted from the pony's lips, long brown hairs that curved back against Shawnee's mouth. It wasn't that she was disgusted. Shawnee was just an ordinary horse smelling of sweat and ammonia who spent her time eating and rolling in the dust and sleeping.

The time when she would have gotten up at dawn, full of excitement, to ride Shawnee across the fields was passed. It was too late for her to see Shawnee as more than an animal to be fed and watered and brushed, with hooves to be cleaned with a pick.

When she and Martha had made up stories about the family who lived in the log cabin, when they had imagined how it would be riding their horses side by side, the pictures had been full of color and excitement. Somehow, the way she had imagined it, the horses were like those in the movies, prancing across fields of amazing green. Horse, rider, earth, and sky all part of the same glorious thing.

But now, riding Shawnee by herself, she discovered it wasn't like that. She was aware of the stiffness of the saddle between her legs; she kept an eye out for rocks so Shawnee wouldn't stumble. There was only the sunlight—too bright—and the midges dancing. No excitement or magic illumined anything she did anymore. She'd tried a few times to talk to Shawnee, but she'd only felt silly. It was impossible even to pretend that Shawnee understood what was said to her. Wherever she went now or whatever she did it was just her own mind, shut up in a narrow place, talking to itself.

By herself she couldn't make up games any longer, and so she put away the mother and the father dolls, the ones who had occupied the log cabin for so many years. She put the girl with long hair and the girl with short curly hair with them, putting all the family in a box that she stuck behind her socks. Before she put them away she looked at the dolls with cold eyes and saw that they were imperfectly painted and some of the paint had spread onto their hands and into their hair. She didn't even like to look at them anymore.

She had seen her grandmother's house as a place where sunlight lay over the roses painted on the linoleum, where people smiled across the breakfast table and there were always arms to cradle you from any bad thing. But now she knew that had always been a lie. That bright world was the one that only babies knew.

She went to school alone and came home alone, the journey spanned by the trip in the yellow school bus as it had been in the other house. But it was not the same.

She was in sixth grade, still in the square brick building where the first-graders went. It wouldn't be until next year that she would go to the low, sprawling high school building. But the other girls in her class put on lipstick secretly in the restroom, rubbing it off on a paper towel before they went into the hall again. At recess they still played tag and running base sometimes, but they often sneaked over to the high school grounds to watch the boys play baseball.

The others all knew about the terrible thing that had happened in her family and she saw them sometimes, looking at her as they whispered behind their hands, their eyes bright as squirrels'. But it didn't matter. She would have been set apart anyway.

When she came home from school she went to the barn and sometimes she took Shawnee out for a ride, loping her around and around the pasture so Shawnee wouldn't get fat and short of wind. Then she would take off the saddle and bridle and let Shawnee browse over the thin grass. Lying with her head pillowed on her arm, she would shut her eyes against the sun. But open or shut, her eyes saw only what was there. The sweat dark on Shawnee's flanks, the ants running frantically through the weeds. There was no escape from what was. Wherever she went or whatever she did this would not change, no matter what happened to her in her life.

Lenora

WHEN Burl wanted to rent that house, the one on Route 3 with the long driveway leading to it, she'd gone along though her heart was against it. Her heart, in fact, had faltered in her breast. But she wanted to put the past behind them the same as Burl did. A new start in a new place. She understood that. She told herself it might work too— they'd be happy again after all their trials. Hard work might be all it would take.

So she held her doubts in the back of her mind. But she tried, she surely did. Killing herself, practically, to please Burl.

What did he want her to fix for his supper? Anything he was pining for especially? Sure, she'd be glad to pull off the old wallpaper in their bedroom even though the dust got in her nose and made her sneeze. She just put her hair back in a scarf and worked away, never complaining.

She didn't even trouble Burl by telling him how lonesome she got out there in that house by herself, with him at the lumber mill and Adele at school. For two weeks she endured it—the country quiet that she filled as best she could with the noise of her labors. But there was no shutting out her thoughts which, instead of easing, grew worse and worse. She was going to grieve herself to death out there, covered with the dust of ages, and nobody would even hear.

So when one of her cousins, Sally Ann Foster, told her she could use her real well in her beauty shop in Fayetteville—one of her regulars was out having a baby—Lenora jumped at the chance. Heaven-sent. She didn't care what anybody else might have to say on the subject. If she spent her days alone much longer, she was going to be as crazy as poor Jeff and they'd have to put her in alongside of him in that institution. Being with other people again would save her if anything could.

And her spirits did lift the morning she got up to drive to Sally Ann's shop. The moment she walked into the place she knew she'd fit in just fine. One beauty shop was a lot like all the others— a little world of its own—the talk comfortable and soothing, a murmur like a song going on all day. As long as she was there with the other women, she felt a whole lot better.

It was later on, driving home, that she got real blue. As soon as she climbed in the car her heart felt so heavy she could hardly stand it. Her grief over Martha came back to her and her grief over Jeff too, left all by himself in that institution. Nobody to visit him except Scott, and she knew better than to put much reliance on him. He was a kind-hearted boy but so wrapped up in his own affairs.

But these griefs, terrible as they were, weren't the only ones she had to suffer. Maybe it was being back in a beauty shop again that brought the other one back to her full force. The shameful grief. The one she couldn't tell a soul about. But there it was, not to be denied any longer: Charles, and wanting him still. He'd been there all along in the back of her mind but held at bay. Biding his time, she saw now.

That very night she dreamed about him again. There he was, smiling, looking so handsome in his suede jacket, holding out his hand to her.

And there he came, night after night, his arms close around her, whispering in her ear. "My sweet whore. Sweet little Nore."

She gave herself good talkings-to in the mornings as she drove to work, carrying on such conversations with herself that anybody passing her on the road might think she was a crazy woman. It couldn't have gone on much longer with Charles anyway; it was a doomed affair and had no future from the start. But whatever she said, it didn't do any good; she might as well have been talking to the wind. In spite of all she could do, sometimes she just let go and said, "Oh Charles, Oh Charles," over and over like her heart would break. How was she going to get through the rest of her life without Charles to love? She was like somebody given a life sentence.

Being alone with Burl during those evenings after supper made her frantic. He drove her wild going on and on about what color they ought to paint the house. He could paint it purple for all she cared. As far as she was concerned they could live somewhere in a tent. None of that mattered at all.

If somebody put a hand plow in her hands and set her loose on the garden plot, she'd go about breaking up the ground all by herself, working until she was ready to drop, worn to a frazzle. Her only hope was to crawl into bed so tired she would fall into exhausted sleep. About like hitting herself over the head with a hammer every day.

What scared her so bad was that she didn't think she could go on without something to look forward to. She was only thirty-eight, not that old a woman, and it was like a lid had come down, sealing her up in a box so there was no way out.

Shameful. Oh, she knew it. But she didn't care anymore.

All the time on those drives in the early morning, through countryside all soft with spring, she was saying, "I just can't go on like this. If not Charles, then somebody else. Only somebody, you hear me? If you won't let me have love, then just forget it. Keep the rest. If you won't give me love you might as well kill me right here. Go on, strike me dead right here in the middle of the highway. I don't care."

God wouldn't do it, though, and it was no use depending on Him. Anybody who had let an innocent child be killed the way He had was not somebody prepared to help. No fairness or sense in any of it as far as she could see.

If not God, then there should be something else. Something beyond God, something she couldn't put a name to out there somewhere.

But all she knew was love.

Jeff

Her face was the face of an angel, pure, the fine white skin, the lips holding that blush of pink. Under her eyelids it was blue. He could see the blue of her eyes through the skin thin as paper, her eyes looking up, watching something he could not see.

The sound of wings, the rushing of wind. He had known the breath on his back, had felt it stir the hair on the nape of his neck as he leaned forward to see, to hear. At the moment of her passing the vision would be given to him. He would sweep into the void further than he had ever gone, beyond any point of reference, beyond every cell making up him, him, Jeff. There would be no more left of Jeff than there was of water remaining on sand where the sun has fallen, hot, sucking up all moisture, leaving nothing but the dried grains of sand, desiccated.

And in that void—absent utterly from himself,

spirit only and perhaps not even spirit but only the kind of awareness a tree has—he would know the mystery. He would be given the secret that had to be torn in the passing from one state to another. For that time he would be joined with his sister, his spirit linked to hers. For that instant only, he would be flooded with light, with overwhelming knowledge. He would bask in that vision that the dying strained to see, that which could not be expressed in human tongue. He would see the veil of heaven rent, "and behold, a door was opened in heaven: and the first voice which I heard was as it were of a trumpet talking with me. . . ."

He would understand the beatitude on the faces of the newly dead, would know why, at the last moment, their lips curved upward into a smile of delight, of joy inexpressible.

When she grew still under his hands he felt the spirit of her passing like a breath of wind, and he lifted the pillow from her face with the care he would have used opening the seal of the holy of holies. In that moment the faint echo of her joy would come to him and he would be forever in a state of beatitude, of grace everlasting. He would know the alpha and the omega.

Let me know, oh, my little sister, tell me what you know, what you see, let the mystery be opened to me too, and I will know the only thing I will ever want to know. I will have the only knowledge worth living for.

And when he had lifted away the pillow from her face, opening out in that final joy so it filled his eyes, he saw as from a great distance the explosion of light that had seared his inner eyes shut forever, that had burned itself like fire into his human brain, too frail a device to hold it, and it was all he knew or wanted to know. He was content, having the only thing he had ever wanted—was content and would be forever and ever.

Amen.

Mary Elsie Robertson was born and raised in Charleston, Arkansas, and was educated at the University of Arkansas and the University of Iowa. She was the recipient of the Mademoiselle *College Fiction Prize for one of the stories in her first book,* Jordan's Stormy Banks, *published by Atheneum in 1961. Since then she has written two children's books and two other novels. She has had fellowships at both MacDowell and Yaddo writers' colonies, and has been awarded a fellowship for 1983 by the National Endowment for the Arts. Her short fiction has appeared in several magazines, including* Ms., Redbook, The Virginia Quarterly, *and* New England Review. *She has taught at the State University of New York at Brockport, and lives in upstate New York.*